Cascarones

Sylvia Sánchez Garza

Crimson Cardinal Press

 Crimson Cardinal Press

Edinburg, Texas
crimsoncardinalpress.com

ISBN-13: 979-8-9884810-3-4
ISBN-ebook: 979-8-9884810-0-3
Library of Congress Control Number: 2024907848

Made in the USA

Cascarones

Table of Contents

This book is dedicated to my best friend, my sister, the general, Ana. You are always in our hearts and so deeply missed. Love you forever Annie!

The Golden Egg

"Black dresses—check, black pumps—check, black sunglasses—check, extra Kleenex—check, and of course don't forget the blessed *Rosario*—check..." Diana says to herself thinking that no one heard her.

As *Tía* Julia told everyone at the last *Rosario*, "We're all trained when it comes to funerals." Heck, we pretty well had the drill down.

Sadly, we had been experiencing these unwelcome family reunions way too often. First, was the farewell at the funeral home. Then, the *misa* at Santa Juana Catholic Church followed. Lastly, was the procession to the burial at the cemetery for the final *despedida* complete with the *mariachis,* "*Volver, Volver.*" Sometimes, there would be a combo gun salute with the *mariachis*, if the loved one was a veteran.

The only upside for the *familia*—it was a perfect time to catch up with out of town relatives. Funerals and weddings both offered the opportunity for family gatherings. Since many of the *primos* had now started to grow up and move away, these were the events that brought everyone together. When we were younger, we would always get together. Now only certain occasions brought us back home.

"Stay gold," she said as we were driving home from Weslaco on the way back from our *primo*'s funeral. We had arrived just in the nick of time. Of course we had made it to the *Rosario* the night before as expected; but as *primas*, we had to see his face one final time. For family it was important, and unfortunately it had become a familiar event for both of us.

"What are you talking about?" I asked my sister as I threw off my four-inch-high heels that were killing me and tried to get comfortable in the passenger seat of her Astrovan. She was the one driving, always in control. I absolutely hated driving, and she knew that.

"You remember. Stay gold, like Johnny in *The Outsiders*."

That was her favorite poem, and the fact that it came up in that novel made her love it even more. We had both taught it to our students while teaching at the local high school.

"I know Di, but why are you even bringing that up?"

Being part of a close-knit Mexican American, Rio Grande Valley family, my brothers, sisters, and I grew up with the privilege of always being surrounded by loved ones regardless of where we were. Our fifty plus first cousins on Mommy's side, and almost thirty first cousins on Daddy's side were like brothers and sisters to us. All of the family celebrations included them.

"Don't you see? In a way, he was Johnny! That's why..."

I look at my sister with a blank stare, who is only two years older than me, but has always been so much wiser, even though I'd never dare tell her that ...as she continues to talk to me about our *primo* Jimmy who was only twenty-five years old. Why did we have to say goodbye so soon?

"*¡Ay, Dios Mío!* You need to get over here right now. Something terrible has happened to Jimmy." I could barely make out the sobbing words on the other end of the phone early that dreadful morning, when Mommy called me only a few days before. She didn't give me details, except for us to hurry up and get to *Tío* Milo's house in Weslaco. She didn't have to say anything; in my heart, I knew something was horribly wrong. I quickly planned, nervously awaited by the door for what seemed hours to be picked up by my sister Di, and we did as were told.

As we traveled along the busy expressway trying our best not to speed, we passed all of the cars and pickup trucks along the way, moving in slow motion. As we drove by the holiest place in the Valley, The Basílica de la Virgen de San Juan, we looked at each other, but didn't say a word. This, the Holy City of the Virgin, where we would always go to get holy water and special blessings, was now making us feel forgotten. Thousands of people of all denominations from all over the world visit our very own *Basílica*. Since we were young children, we were taught that out of respect, we had to bless ourselves with a sign of the cross as we passed. *En el nombre Del Padre, Del Hijo, y Del Espíritu Santo*. Not today. Usually, we would talk nonstop about anything. Today, we didn't feel like talking.

When we finally arrived at my *tía* and *tío's* neighborhood where my *primo* Jimmy lived, all of our cousins, *tías* and *tíos* were already there. The cars were all lined up along the narrow, dirt road that led to the dreaded, somber house. Shaking and terrified of the inevitable news we were about to receive... We unbuckled our seatbelts and proceeded to get bombarded by everyone. We slowly walked towards the house and hesitantly went up the three wooden steps, entered the crowded frame home through the side door by the open garage, and sure enough were swarmed with red, bloodshot eyes staring at us, while mouths quickly moved, but didn't say anything. Our *primas* were trying desperately to tell us the worst possible news, which not even the *Rosario* that I was carrying seemed to shield us from.

"It's Jimmy; he's gone!" Our *prima* Bibi finally cried out. "How could he? How could he?" She continued to mumble over and over to herself…

Nothing else was said, but it was clear to us what had happened. Why was it that our handsome *primo*, our protector, so full of life, had decided to go through with this? It just couldn't be. Yet, there in a dark corner of the room sat my *Tío* Milo shattered to his core, trying but not able to hold up his sobbing face. In that one day it seemed that he aged countless years, for his life had been sucked right out of him, blank, nothing left. As he looked up at me for a brief second he cried, *"Se nos fue mi Jimmy, m'ija..."*

"HEY! SUZY! ARE YOU LISTENING TO ME? Did you hide them? Are all of them hidden?"

Keki almost blew my ear off yelling at me in her shrieking voice sounding like a blaring siren, forcing me to join everyone in the action and reality happening around me.

"Yes, Yes! I already hid them. They won't be able to find those, don't worry. There is NO WAY that they will find "that" one this year. Not without help."

Just then, water begins to cool my face, as Isaac's pudgy little toddler feet splash me. Giggling in his adorable laugh, everyone grabs their cell phones to capture the moment. For some reason he thinks that splashing his *tías* and messing up their perfect shots is hilarious, so he continues to kick his *patitas*, and we of course let him soak us.

"Look over here Baby—¡*Otro*! Smile!" Trying to get his attention on the opposite end of the pool are Keki and Eli, with some of the kids, waving and making funny faces at him like the cute animal YouTube videos, except they look ridiculous. "Over here—Cheese!"

Basking in the moment, Mommy and Daddy are sitting on cushioned patio chairs in awe of their only great-grandson. They are the perfect pair. No one would ever be able to tell that they have been through so many hardships in their almost eighty years, and of those, nearly sixty together. We don't blame them for seeing him, the youngest one, as "special," the "golden child."

Although years have now passed since his grandmother left us, she must know him. He is so much like her. While the one who he thinks is his grandmother is his great-grandmother continues to ooh and awe over him, everyone's thoughts are surely of her. What would have been? As the grandchildren circle around him like hummingbirds around a red hibiscus bush, they await the greatly anticipated egg hunt.

The new generation of cousins' ranges in age from eleven to twenty-five, yet that seems to be irrelevant since they all get along so well and have built a close-knit bond with each other. They can go months without seeing each other, and when they reunite it's as if they had never been apart. The oldest, Philip, is the leader of the pack and Isaac's dad. He towers over him like a proud papa bear protecting his cub. Husky and grisly with his long hair tied back in a neat ponytail. His tan color contrasts his baby's extremely fair skin. The other kids then come after him all the way down to the eleven-year-olds. All of them unique and so different, yet they all fit into the same puzzle. The generations have changed, but the close-knit family bond is still strong.

First things first though, the heat is unbearable in the Valley, so they must first throw each other into the swimming pool to cool off from the 100-degree temperature. They are all now like little kids trick or treating and absolutely no age difference separating them. Living in South Texas, pool parties have become part of the *cascarón* culture at Easter. It just gets too darn hot—unbelievably hot, thanks perhaps to our ever-changing global climate. Since I'm the *tía* with the pool, now the traditional Easter Egg Hunt has made its way to our home. The hunt hasn't changed by any means. It's still as it always has been, which is why it's so prevalent in our family anyway.

"I'm doing the golden again this year. Which one are you going to do so that I can tell Keki?" Mommy calls me asking me about the hunt.

"It doesn't matter; I can do the bronze one." I take the bronze one as I do every year. Still, Mommy goes through the motions and asks us any way to see if we want to change.

"Fine then, I'll tell Keki that she's doing the silver one. We'll need to start looking for big eggs. Not regular eggs, we need really big eggs." Mommy gets very excited with the Easter hunt every year, and this year will be the first one that Isaac will be able to participate, so it will be extra special.

"I know Mommy; I'll be looking out for jumbo eggs."

The golden egg used to be my sister's egg, but now Mommy does that one. It was always a tradition for my older sister to do the GOLD egg. It was her responsibility, and she loved being in charge of the highlight of our festivities.

Everything is now different, but it is Easter and a time of rebirth and renewal. Now, this time will be the first that Isaac will be looking for that special egg.

"Diana would be absolutely crazy right now with that baby!"

Mommy drifts off into her little world remembering her oldest daughter who was gone way too early. It's hard for me also. Years pass…and it doesn't get any better, but we move forward.

"You know Mommy; I think he does know her somehow, and she has to know him."

"Yes, you're right," she says, and then there's just silence.

All the cousins search for the coveted golden egg as if they were searching for "The Holy Grail." It doesn't matter what's inside of it; it's the principle. It's the fact that it is the "Golden One." Sometimes it takes hours to find, but no one gives up until it is found. Of course there is the silver, and the bronze as well, but the significance is of no comparison. The one who finds the impossibly, incredibly well hidden, golden egg is always the hero of the day. Usually this almost impossible task can only be undertaken by the older cousins. Even then, they typically need hints to help them out. Through the years, they have figured out that this prize is not just any prize, and it will not be hidden in any ordinary hiding place.

Once, Daddy hid it inside a bag of fertilizer that was under a bunch of old pots in the far corner of the yard where no one ever dared to go because sometimes snakes hid there, and it had been wrapped up in some crumpled papers. Another time, it was under the ragged blankets and torn up pillow that were deep inside of our not too friendly guard dog's house directly behind his favorite collection of half-eaten chew toys. Regardless, *cascarones* are on hold until then.

After the golden is found, the *cascarón* king or queen is crowned, and pictures are taken. The winner proudly poses with the trophy as one by one everyone pulls out his phone to snap a quick photo. It is then that the glorious egg is passed around for everyone to envy.

"Ooooh! Aaaah! Check it out!"

Cries are heard as it travels from sweaty hand to sweaty hand.

"Next year it's mine!"

All of the other cousins vow that come next Easter they will be the ones to find that evasive egg.

"Yes, you will be mine!" They all claim.

Then, the festivities of *cascarón* cracking begin. Everyone by now is well trained to wait until all the cousins are ready as if they were auditioning for a play. They have all done this many times before, sometimes three or four times a year. At school there is usually an egg hunt, but that one has too many rules. Then, at the other grandmother's house there is also an egg hunt, but some of the cousins don't believe in Easter, so they don't all participate. Also, the neighborhood sometimes has one for the kids, but they really don't hide the eggs; they just throw them in the grass, so that's not fun. So, this egg hunt is the one that everyone truly looks forward to.

It is then that the action transcends upon the lawn, and a rainbow of confetti explodes into the sky like Skittles pouring down everyone's heads blended in with beads of colored sweat. Blurs of cousins, *tías*, grandmas, friends, and dogs pass before ones' eyes with high pitched shrieks of laughter mixed in with the screams of joy as well as the occasional bark, and miraculously it's over—just like that. The yard instantly turns into a psychedelic sea of paper dots and a mosaic masterpiece of colored eggshells. Definitely, this is the climax of the Easter festivities—getting eggs cracked on your head.

Yet, they have changed a bit throughout the years, but we cannot forget that we do get together at this time to remember that Jesus sacrificed His life so that all of us could have eternal life. Family and getting together are still the most important part after celebrating Easter mass together, which is how we always begin our Easter Sunday mornings. And yes, our Easter celebrations have always included *cascarones*. After all, eggs have always meant new life, spring, and a new beginning. However, our Easters' weren't always about *cascarones*, swimming, and golden eggs. After Easter mass, they used to be solely about *cascarones*, well mostly *cascarones*...

Easter Sunday was always an extra special day for us. Being raised Catholic in Weslaco, a small South Texas town in the Rio Grande Valley, attending mass always started these blessed mornings.

The night before, Mommy would tell us, "Get your clothes ready for tomorrow!"

Diana, Keki, and I would get our Easter dresses, shoes, and hats ready by laying them out on our dresser so that they would be prepared for us to put on in the morning. We'd also get our play clothes ready for the egg hunt so that we would have those available for after church. We would have to come home and change quickly to make it to the park where all of our family would be.

"I'll take a shower first; then you guys can go next. Y'all always take forever in there."

My big sister started giving orders like a general in charge of her soldiers. She loved telling us what to do and how to do it.

"Fine—hurry up!"

Banging on the wooden door, Keki and I would sit outside the one bathroom with our pajamas in our hands until Diana would get out.

"Finally!"

After our showers, the three of us would go to bed early by cuddling up in the bed we shared, so we could be up with the sun. We were a sandwich of sisters with Keki always getting the middle. She was the ham, and we were the bread so that she wouldn't fall out or get scared.

"You have to!" We'd tell her. "Or else you'll fall off."

Keki hated being the ham, but that's how it was since she was the baby girl. She said she hated being the baby, but she must have liked it because everyone always wanted to touch her golden curls. Why was her hair full of curls when ours was straight as a board?

"¡*Ay, qué chula,* baby!"

The *tías* always went on and on about how cute Keki was with her bouncing curls. My hair was a boring flat *tabla*.

We'd get dressed up in our pretty dresses, our brothers in their nice shirts, and load up in our Batmobile to Easter mass bright and early.

"Hurry up!"

Mommy would rush us because our church would get so packed that if you didn't get there thirty minutes early you would have to stand up in the back. Everyone in church would be dressed in nice clothes, and the ladies in church would all wear *velos* on their head. Girls were always taught to wear dresses in church, and boys had to wear their best clothes.

In this church, every family seemed to have their designated pew. The seven of us would go straight up to the front of the church and file into pew number four on the right-hand side occupying the entire space, which we claimed as our very own. We would all kneel down, do the sign of the cross, and pray. Sometimes, it would be for one second and Mommy would give us a look. Then, we'd quickly kneel back down and pray longer.

"Why do you have to wear that, Mommy?"

She used to have different ones in her top drawer in different styles and colors for church. Sometimes she would wear a black with gold and sometimes a whitish one.

"It's respectful for women to cover their heads, now shhh!"

We would sit in church just waiting and hoping for the time to come for us to leave for our Easter Egg Hunt while Mommy and Papi yelled at us with their eyes.

"Is it almost time? Is it almost time? Is it almost time? Is it almost time?"

"¡Ya, cállense!"

The mass would seem as if it took forever for us, until—finally! The final blessing came, and we would go home to change and let the fun begin.

Our favorite place to celebrate Easter was at my *Tío* Rolando's (*El* Red's). He had taken a job for the county as caretaker for the best park in the Valley, Sunrise Hill. This was where all of our cousins would get together after Easter mass for a barbeque and Easter Egg Hunt. We were the luckiest ones in the Valley because my *tío* and *tía* lived there. Their kids, our eight cousins, had access to any part of the park that we wanted to go to.

"Are we almost there? Are we almost there? Are we there yet? Are we almost there?"

We'd all be asking *Papi* as we'd be getting closer to the park. Sunrise Hill was pretty far away from our house, since it was at the other end of the county. It must've taken hours to drive all the way over. As we got closer, the anticipation was evident in our faces.

"I hope I don't get all of the raw eggs this year," Diana said.

"Forget that! As long as you don't get the flour after the raw ones," Johnny added.

"You don't even have hair!" I shouted at him.

"That's enough!" Mommy yelled at us. Do you want to do the *cascarones* or not?

"YES! YES! YES!!!" We all yelled. Then we'd start with "¡¡¡*Cascarones, cascarones, cascarones*!!!"

"Well then, you'll have to take the raw and the flour too. That's just the way it is."

We hated the raw eggs and the flour *cascarones*. We never used those kinds of eggs.

Mommy only made the confetti eggs. She was quite proud of her artistic *cascarones*. All year long we would save the eggshells every time that we used eggs. Mommy taught us how to crack them with only tapping the top edge of the egg. Then we would wash them, dry them, and put them away on the top cabinet in the kitchen. During the year we would make confetti by cutting out little tiny paper circles from the newspaper funnies. About a month before Easter, we would start dying and decorating the eggshells, filling them with the confetti, and gluing the ends with a piece of paper. This was a yearlong project, but we loved it, and it was well worth it. Our finished products, the *cascarones*, were masterpieces.

Mommy and the *tías* would compare each other's *cascarones* to see which ones were the prettiest. We were so proud of them, yet we knew that they had to be smashed on people's heads. That was their purpose.

Mommy would explain to us how the egg symbolized life.

"All of you start out as an egg. The *cascarón*, although beautifully decorated and exquisitely adorned, started as an egg. Now it is a mere shell, like us. What matters is what we have inside. *Lo que es importante es el espíritu que tienen adrento.* Once the shell cracks, it goes back to the earth and helps to fertilize plants so it never really dies."

Not all of the kids that went to the park used confetti. Many took a shortcut and used flour. I guess they thought it was faster and fun for them. We didn't like the way it stuck to our hair especially when some weirdos would use raw eggs to crack on our heads. That wasn't fun at all. It never failed, some of them would get raw eggs to break, and then the others would come and crack flour eggs smack on the freshly shampooed head. Then you had to stay with egg, flour and confetti stuck to your hair until the end of the day. Even by putting it up in a ponytail, it was still gross. The worst part was that when we would finally get home; there was only one bathroom, which meant only one shower, and we'd have to wait until it was our turn to use it. With seven in the family, sometimes the wait would be pretty long. Other than that, it was Disneyworld at Sunrise Hill. We absolutely loved it!

"They're here! They're here!" The Rentería cousins came out of the house yelling as our car pulled up the long gravel drive towards their temporary home. Going to their place was always an automatic party because they were a family of ten including my *Tía* Marta and *Tío* Red. We always thought that we had a huge family, but they had a really huge family.

My cousins were Role, Monny, Mireya, Mati, Minerva, Meli, Zelinda, and Rafael in that order. The boys were all R names (Monny's name was Ramón, but everyone called him Monny for short), and the girls' names were all M names except for the youngest girl Zelinda. We don't know what happened when she was born. I guess my *tía* and *tío* ran out of M girl names that they liked, and just went for the Z.

They were so lucky because they lived at the best park in the Valley with so many trees and rolling hills. There were several recreation areas for us to play at and many barbecue, canopies, and picnic areas as well. Everything surrounded them, and on Easter Sunday the entire family including most of the fifty cousins gathered to celebrate at their home. After our arrival, all of the other cousins started arriving and unloading their goods.

"*Ten*, Roli *llévate la* potato salad *para adentro y ponla en la hielera. Pablo baja los cascarones*," my *Tía* Inéz would tell my cousins.

One by one the *tías* would take their delicious goodies inside the house and put them away to be enjoyed later. The *cascarones* would get stacked outside the house in a designated area where the adults would then hide them, after the *tías* had inspected them. The kids would all take off to play. We always had dozens and dozens of them that would take forever to find, but it was so much fun.

Once all of the cousins arrived, it was time to roll down the hills…

"Let's go to the top of the hill!"

We'd all run to the biggest hill and line up rolling down like stones. Covered in grass and stickers we'd run up the hill and do it again. Some of us would lie down in a row, tuck our hands in by our hips and then get pushed. The boy cousins were always more daring; they'd tuck their knees up to their chins, wrap their arms around themselves and take off head first. My sisters, Diana, Keki, and I all had long hair, so naturally it would tangle easily when we'd play on the hill and get covered with grass. Today, we couldn't get in trouble though because our parents were busy talking with the *tías* and *tíos*. The dads were barbecuing, and the moms were on *cascarón* duty while getting the rest of the food ready; they didn't have time to worry about us. It was the perfect day to play with no worries.

"What a great day to roll down the hills!"

All of us were laughing and playing, not even caring about getting our hair tangled, just running up the hill and having a blast. As we all got to the top of the hill again, we stopped laughing. We just froze. Out of nowhere three big kids popped up at the top of the hill where all of us were and stared us down. Their eyes shot at us like a squirt of evil. With a mean look on their faces they started to tell us some things that we couldn't understand too clearly, but I'm sure they were bad words. We definitely weren't allowed to say those kind of words. Some we had never even heard.

"Hey! *Qué Onda*? You guys think you own this park or what?"

The boy was obviously the leader of the group, standing a bit in front of the other two. He was tall and heavyset with long hair that went past his neckline.

"We were here first so we get to use this hill. You *vatos* have to go play somewheres else."

He pushed his way closer so that he could get a better look and stared right into my guy cousin's eyes. Thank goodness they were with us.

"Hey! What's the matter with you all? Can't you see our girl cousins are here? This is no place for a fight."

My cousin, Role, the oldest of the Rentería clan was tough looking with his long hair. His hair was the nice kind of soft hair not messy like the mean guy's hair. He, his brother Monny, Johnny, and my younger cousin Jimmy, were together and obviously these other guys knew them.

"Well, we're not leaving... This is our hill. Take your little cousins and get otta here, bros."

"Órale bro! It's Easter, man! *No seas así*. This is Sunrise Hill; we can all use it."

Role, the pacifist was trying to calm them down and work things out as he approached the leader putting his hand on his shoulder.

"C'mon Mando…we don't want to fight. Check it out; it's a beautiful day. How about we share it?"

Monny was holding Jimmy back telling him to settle down as we watched. It never took much to get Jimmy all riled up, and when something did…he became a little firecracker. Many times, my little *primo* would let his little temper get the best of him at school, and if one of the other *primos* weren't around to calm him down then he'd end up getting into trouble that could've easily been avoided. We knew him all too well, and we didn't want to have to call my *Tío* Milo to get him and risk having that drama play out for all to see. My poor *Tío* knew the drill with my *primo* all too well. Yes, he was a fighter, but he was also a charmer who could always light up any room—a little sunbeam.

"How come you always want to fight, yet you're so sweet?" We'd always ask him.

"I don't want to fight; I just have to defend my *primas*." At school, he'd always look out for all of us and try to protect us.

Before we knew it…a crowd had gathered around us on the hill cheering Jimmy on.

"Fight! Fight! Fight! Fight!" They chanted with their hands waving up in the air.

Several of the kids from school were there, and so were many that we had never seen before.

"Fight! Fight! Fight! Fight!"

"Where did everyone come from?" I stepped towards Jimmy and shook my head in disapproval. "You better not do anything."

He yanked his arm free from Monny's grip to everyone's screams of approval.

"¡*Yo no me dejo*!" He yelled out to the crowd.

"Oh boy, here we go!" I told myself.

"Jimmy! NO!" I yelled at him as he turned and looked at me in a surprised look. "Please don't fight with these guys; we'll all get in trouble."

I tried pleading with him while Diana and Keki pulled me back because it was getting obvious that he was going to fight regardless of what any of us did or said.

Standing on top of the hill, we could see everything going on in the park. In a distance were our parents, *tíos*, and *tías* sitting around the barbecue pit talking and laughing who knows about what…oblivious to what was happening on the hill. To the other side were other families doing the same thing. Scattered within the park were other groups cracking their *cascarones*, running and laughing; that would have been us, but now here we were about to witness a fight for no reason.

"I'm going to run and call *Tío* Milo."

I quickly turn around to run down the hill where the family was as I feel a firm tug on my shirt.

"NO! Don't go. That'll just make things worse for all of us."

Diana and Role were both telling me not to go. As I look up at them, they both shake their heads in disapproval at me. "What did I do? I'm just trying to help!" Left with no choice, I had to listen to them. They were the oldest ones.

"FIGHT! FIGHT! FIGHT!"

The crowd kept yelling on top of the hill. For sure our parents could hear.

Mando, the leader of the mean guys came right up to Jimmy and stood face to face with him, staring at him as if he wanted to eat him. Of course, Jimmy had to look up to look at him in the face, since Mando was so much taller than he was, but that didn't matter to him one bit. He was so much bigger than Jimmy that most kids would have run, but that didn't stop my *primo* from trying to punch his face in. As Jimmy shot him a fierce glare back and then picked up his fist about to swing it at his face, Mando stopped him.

"Hey! Wait a minute *vato*—it's true you know—it is Easter. Maybe we shouldn't fight."

Now he started to back away a bit.

"What's the matter with you man? Are you chicken?" Jimmy seemed confused at what was happening.

"Come on man put'em up! What are you waiting for? Let's give these people a show. That's what they're waiting for."

18

As he stood there ready to punch his nemesis, Mando just seemed to smile back at him. He really did want to fight but at the same time he felt a bit of relief, and a bittersweet feeling overcame him…

"So, what do you want to do then?"

Mando looked out at the crowd, then at Jimmy, and then at us. The crowd was anxiously waiting for action, a fight or something to happen.

"A challenge." Mando says.

"A challenge?" All of us look confused.

What were these guys talking about? They didn't seem like the type to call for challenges, but here we were about to accept a dare from them.

"We get to hunt the *cascarones* with you guys. If we find more, then we win. We also get to use our kind of *cascarones*."

"What kind do y'all use?"

I had to ask because who knows with these guys.

"You'll find out soon enough." Mando said, as he laughed with his buddies. "What do say *vatos*? Deal?"

My cousins looked at each other. They didn't want to fight and cause the family to get upset with them during the Easter celebration, so it was pretty much a no-brainer.

"It's a deal!" The crowd started to leave in disappointment, and the hill began to empty.

All of us ran down the hill and back to our headquarters to see if it was time for us to hunt for the *cascarones*. By now everyone else had arrived. All of the *primos*, *tías*, and *tíos* were there, and they were all waiting for us.

"Where have y'all been?" My cousin Bibi started questioning us.

She could tell something was going on because we were with Mando, and she knew who he was from school. As she came up to me to get the scoop, I motioned to her that everything was fine.

"Everyone, these are our friends, and they're going to hunt for *cascarones* with us."

Role, Johnny, and Diana introduced the guys to all of the adults so that they wouldn't be wondering who they were.

Waves and hellos were quickly exchanged.

Turning around, I reached down for my basket that was by the front door next to all of the other colorful Easter baskets. I knew which one was mine because I had pulled some of the pink straw out of the handle, and it was sticking straight up like a sharp pink spear waiting to hurt someone accidentally.

Grasping it, I ran and almost bumped right into Mando.

"Oh, are you looking for your basket?"

He looked at me like I had just come from some strange planet or something.

"Are you kidding? We don't do baskets."

I looked right up at him holding my pink basket in my hand. By now everyone else was grabbing his basket as well. "How can you hunt for *cascarones* without a basket? Where are you gonna put the *cascarones*?"

Mando stuck his hand in his Levi's front pocket and pulled out a large, folded, crinkled, brown paper bag.

"Don't worry about it."

Tía Marta came out of the house to tell us the boundaries of where the *cascarones* were hidden. "The rules are there are no rules." Baskets and bags were in hand and everyone was off.

"I found a bunch over here in these bushes!" The first yells came from the distance and then others could be heard.

"In the trees—look in the trees!"

We looked up, and we looked down the many hiding places inside of boxes and cans, under cars, behind things, on top of places. The possibilities were limitless. *Cascarones* were everywhere, even hidden throughout the grass where the *tías* and *tíos* were sitting. All of the baskets and bags were beginning to get full. The time had finally come to see who had collected more *cascarones*, them or us?

"NO ONE CRACK YET!!!" Johnny yelled out. "We need to see who has more eggs."

All of the *primos* gathered around Johnny, Role, and Diana and started to count everyone's *cascarones*. Mando's group did the same. It was evident that we had more than Mando's group. Then all of a sudden, a smaller version of Mando popped out of nowhere and brought him two huge tubs of eggs.

"Wait *vatos*—these are mine too!"

All of us were just looking at the eggs as if there were snakes in that basket. There may as well have been.

"WHAT!!!"

"No fair! Y'all didn't find those. You had to find them. That was the challenge!" All of us were yelling at them.

"¡*Cálmensen vatos*! Remember *La Tía* said, The Rule is there are no rules! My friend just found these eggs, so you have to count them."

Jimmy's face was turning red with the afternoon heat and the heat that was building up inside him towards this Mando character. He was about to blow…

"¡Órale! We all know you didn't find those eggs. Just fess up man!"

Starting to go towards him again Mando yelled out, "RULE IS THERE ARE NO RULES!!" and he grabbed some of the raw eggs and cracked them on Jimmy's head!

"Now you did it *vato*!" He then took some of Mando's raw eggs and cracked them on his head.

"I guess this means we won!" Mando yells!

Everyone started cracking eggs on each other's heads. There were raw ones; some with flour in them, and of course our confetti eggs that had been carefully, and beautifully decorated. The flour eggs, confetti eggs, raw eggs, and shells stuck to everyone's hair and clothes and made a terrible mess, but everyone had a great time.

"Who brought these awful eggs anyway?" The *tías* asked.

"Our new friends did." We all answered as we all laughed chasing them to crack the awful eggs on their heads.

All we could hear was, "¡¡Ay!! *Caranchos*!!" as they then grabbed a handful of brightly colored and artistically decorated *cascarones* scrutinizing them.

"Wow! ¡*Chequen le, vatos*! We can't crack these! ¡Órale bros!—*Miren*, this one is beautiful!"

Holding them up to look at the egg in the center of the stack, Mando yells, "Jimmy—Look!"

Jimmy then carefully takes the masterpiece from his friend, holds it up to the sky for all to see.

"Everyone, Check it out. It's Golden!!"

Seven Plus Lobo

The familiar buzzing of the General Electric fan in the kitchen window muffled the sounds of us arguing as we all sat around our small green Formica kitchen table wondering whose turn it was to wash the dishes and sweep the floor. There were seven of us in our family: *Papi*, Mommy, Johnny, Diana, me, Keki, and Eli, plus my dog Lobo. My grandfather had given him to me as a puppy. Johnny was named after *Papi* because that was his name and that was also our grandfather, *Apá* Juan's name. He was the oldest son and oldest grandson. Diana or Diana Lourdes was named after our *Tía* Diana, *Papi's* sister. Keki was a nickname for Karolina because that was hard for us to say. Eli was also a nickname for Eliazar. He was named for *Papi's* nickname Toni and Eliazar from the Bible. Me…I was named just plain Suzy with no middle name. My grandfather, *Papa* Maximiliano, named my puppy Lobo because he said he looked like a wolf, and I always thought he really was one. I loved my dog, one because he was a wolf, and two because my *Papa* gave him to me as a gift. He could have given him to any of my many, many cousins, (fifty some first cousins on my Mommy's side) but he gave him to me so that made him extra special.

Mommy would always tell me, "You see, you are special." I never really felt special. Johnny was the oldest boy, Diana was the oldest girl, Eli was the baby boy, Keki was the baby girl, and me… I was just in the middle—invisible. It was hard for me to feel special, so I guess I just never did, but Mommy kept telling me that I was special.

Mommy and *Papi* met when they were in the third grade and according to Mommy were in love since then.

"I knew then that I was going to marry him; he was meant for me."

They were married when they were both twenty-three years old because they waited for *Papi* to get back from the army, had my older brother a year later, and then every two years had one of us; exactly two years apart. Of course, I was right in the middle, the invisible one—smack dab in the middle.

"I did it last time."

Diana sprang up from her chair; she was a military general, pointing at me and using her authoritative voice. "You have to do it; I have homework to do and besides I helped Mommy with dinner."

Everyone else just kept eating their *fideo con* chicken and beans while I put my spoon down on the table, crossing my arms firmly.

"That's not fair; why can't Johnny do the dishes? He never does them."

Mommy just looked at me with; you know the answer to that question look, as Johnny gave me a smirk. He just loved his role as the oldest and to top it off the oldest boy of our family. *El Mayor.* "That's just not fair—just because he's a boy!"

Just then we heard the sound of *Papi's* car drive up to the house. Actually, the high-pitched yelping of the neighborhood dogs barking in harmony along with Lobo was usually louder than the car, but they were always on cue. He parked the car on the side of the street competing with the purple bougainvillea that was overtaking the curb, directly outside of our bedroom window. Ours was the best bedroom of the three in our house.

There was my parents' bedroom at the end of the hall with a bed that all of us could fit on sometimes, when they'd let us. My brothers' bedroom was right across from our only tiny bathroom. One bathtub with a shower head, a toilet right next to it, and one small sink with a medicine cabinet that had a mirror attached to the wall were all crammed into a closet-sized room. In the mornings, we'd all line up banging on the door waiting for our turn.

"Hurry up! We're gonna be late! ¡*Ándale!*"

They also had bunk beds to jump off of being superheroes, even though they weren't supposed to, just because they were boys, but our room was still much better. My sisters and I shared it as well as the one full-size bed covered with a pink quilt with tiny little flowers that *Mama* had made for us, and the three of us slept on it very comfortably. The head of our bed was pushed up against the window that had a view right out into the street, and we could see our purple bougainvillea come to life reaching up to the sun plus everything and everyone who would come and go. It was so funny when the dogs would end up chasing our neighbors down the street, barking and barking until they were out of sight. We used to stay up laughing and giggling when the dog posse would chase one of our older neighbor's dates around the corner screaming into the darkness, wondering if they'd be back. Windows were always left open because it was so unbelievably hot, our room was still a desert, but sometimes Mommy put a fan in the window, and it helped at least to blow the air around.

In our neighborhood, everyone used the street to park as if it was a parking lot. They didn't have a choice. So... sometimes it was hard to play around the cars because they would get in the way. That never stopped us though; every day and night we would be outside with the neighborhood kids playing in one of our favorite playgrounds—the street.

Papi usually came home late since he took night classes at the local college or had late meetings, and he'd always be exhausted and hungry. Mommy would always try to keep us calm so that we wouldn't bother him. This evening was different though; we could tell. As he walked in, he had a big smile on his face that made him look so happy that he just loosened his red and blue striped tie and threw it onto his chair by the kitchen table. Our *Papi* only thirty-five years old was already the father of five children, and the only breadwinner of our seven-member family. He was Super Man. There was no other father stronger, smarter, handsomer, or better than ours. He was the athletic type, a boxer, a football and baseball player, an army veteran, and a migrant farmworker, but a quiet disciplinarian, rarely did he show emotion. But now, he was confusing us; what did this mean?

The scent of freshly handmade corn *tortillas, fideo con* chicken, and beans lingered in our house, and Mommy had tried to keep it all warm for him on the gas stove. All of us kids ran to meet *Papi* and started to jump on him grabbing his legs not letting him walk.

"We're moving to Houston!" He exclaimed, as he scooped up my baby brother and flung him up to the ceiling.

"*¡Otro! ¡Otro!*" Eli giggled pushing his head up and digging his feet into his chest so that *Papi* could throw him into the air again.

Of course, the baby got his way—always. So, my baby brother was now being tossed up into the air as all of us started to jump up and down with excitement, not even sure what was going on. Up and down, up and down.

"Why are we all jumping?" I thought, but we weren't sure.

"My turn, my turn! Pleeease!" my little sister started as she grabbed *Papi*'s leg.

"*Ya*! That's enough! ¡*Apacígüense*!"

Mommy would get after all of us so that we could settle down.

"You see what you did!"

"It's all your fault!"

"No, you started it!"

"¡*Otro*! ¡*Otro*!" We all started jumping up and down again and yelling as we ran all over the house.

"We're moving to Houston; we're moving to Houston!"

We ran up and down our tiny hallway from bedroom to bedroom. Meanwhile, Mommy quickly rushed to heat up *Papi*'s dinner on the stove and poured him a glass of iced tea into his favorite Flintstones glass. Mommy always saved the jars after we would finish the grape jelly. As she busily went about serving him, he explained the details of his important meeting that he had just returned from. It must have been pretty important because they didn't even care that we were jumping on the sofa and perfectly made beds and throwing the pillows on the floor to climb on top of them. All we kids knew was that we were moving to Houston; wherever that was.

Just like that, we had to leave our home that all of us had grown up in and move to a place that I had never heard. It was too confusing for me. I was only seven at the time, and all I wanted was to stay at home with my neighborhood friends, be able to see all of my cousins, and go to my school with the kids I knew. I didn't want anything to change.

Mommy was pregnant with me when our home was built entirely surrounded by fields. Our house was the first one in the neighborhood. That's what my parents always told me. They moved into the new white frame house with a beautiful porch, three bedrooms, and one bathroom for all of us to share when I was about to be born—*Papi*, Mommy, Johnny, and Diana. My Mommy had to go to another city because the Weslaco hospital wasn't ready yet, so I was born in a clinic in the city right next to ours, Mercedes. *Papi* was now working for the school district and had graduated from college. Before, he worked for the Gas Company and Diana and Johnny got to live in a different house that was much smaller than this one. I never got to know the smaller house on North Texas Boulevard. For me, this was the best house because it was built for me. It was my house. At least that was what I always thought. My house was my little cocoon.

I was proud of my white frame house on the dirt road. It had a wide front porch that was perfect for playing jacks on because the ball would bounce just right. The trees in the front yard were meant for climbing up into, positioned right next to it so that we could easily climb up onto the roof. It was also right on a corner where a street light was attached to an electric pole and all of the bugs would swarm during the night lighting up our house, placing us right at the end of the neighborhood, not in the middle. It was perfect for me. Maybe my brother and sister had known another house, but not me. I only knew my home, my family, the kids from my neighborhood, and my school; it was all that I wanted.

Our idea of fun in those days was playing outside with all of the neighborhood kids in the street and the vast field of John Deere tractors directly across from our house. That was our favorite playground. All of us kids used to run from one cotton gin tractor to another one with dangerous types of blades sticking out of the front of them and wiggle into the drivers' seat to pretend to be farmers plowing fields. It was up to us to invent our fun in our playground. Therefore, we would claim the biggest and prettiest tractor on the lot and climb up on the top of it. The shiny green ones with the tires taller than I was were my favorite ones.

Diana and I would pretend to be racing a tractor race and then quickly jump off and race off to the yellow long funny looking ones with the sharp blades that looked like curly loops. We'd jump from one to another and hide underneath them and between them, so Johnny couldn't find us. He'd get tired and finally go off and play baseball with the other neighborhood boys.

After playing on the tractors we would gather up all the golf balls that would stray onto our play area since many golfers would practice their game out where we lived. Needless to say, we had a great collection of clean golf balls because we'd take them home and wash them and put them away to use for our jacks' games.

There was always so much to do on the corner of Mesquite Drive and Seventh Street and so many games to invent. Bunches of cotton would collect on our dirt street, and we would gather it up, bring it home and listen intently to the stories my parents would tell us of their backbreaking days of picking it up north. To us it was merely a play item, yet to *Papi* and Mommy it was much more. We had heard the stories over and over that they were engraved in our brains. They even took us to pick tomatoes one summer with my *Tío* Rolando, so we could experience what it was like. That was fun. We'd sit in between the rows of tomatoes and eat some of them until someone would come and get mad at us. The hard part was carrying the basket to the big truck to unload it and then starting all over again.

Both my parents grew up in the fields working as laborers picking fruit, cotton, vegetables, and any type of work that the family could find, and they would travel throughout the country to find work, too. Migrant farmworkers missed so much school during that time that it was a miracle that they completed high school and almost unheard of that *Papi* graduated from college, got his master's degree, and was now given an opportunity to work on his Ph.D. in Houston. Not many Mexican Americans were able to accomplish that in the sixties.

Johnny and Diana were older, and they seemed excited to move. Johnny would be entering junior high which would be a major milestone for him. Diana was only two years older than I, but much more mature and always making sure that I knew she was the responsible one.

She and Johnny always played complicated board games together leaving me out because they would say that I was too young, or that the rules were too complex. I would be excluded from their conversations.

"You won't understand. Go play with Keki. Go away! Lobo needs water or food or something."

"Uhgg!"

They thought Houston would be exciting and adventurous, much different than our small, boring town with only one fast food restaurant. They would talk and make their plans about what they were going to do and where they wanted Mommy and *Papi* to take us on the weekends so that we could explore the big city, but they would never let me plan with them.

Johnny set out to our cozy one sofa living room where *Papi* kept our 1966 set of World Book Encyclopedias and reached for the big H. He and Diana took it along with a notebook and pens and went into Mommy's and *Papi's'* room and shut the door thinking that no one could hear their elaborate plans.

"Keki, come on! Follow me."

"What? Where are you taking me?"

"Just come with me."

Running out the back-kitchen door, around our bedroom window, through the front of the house, right outside Mommy's bedroom window we ran.

"What?"

"Shhh, just listen…"

We got as close to the window screen as we could, stepping on Mommy's Esperanzas and Teresitas, smashing them, as I tried to climb onto the Chinaberry tree next to the house. Someone was going to get in trouble for that, especially because the Teresitas were Mommy's favorite. Grabbing the branch so that I could get a closer look we heard a yell.

"What do you think you're doing?"

"Runnn!"

I jumped from the tree, and Keki and I ran as Johnny came out running after us.

"She made me; she made me!"

I could hear Keki crying. Not me, I was used to it. So used to it. *Papi* would always listen to Johnny because he was the oldest, and he was a boy, and he would always tell my sisters and me that we had to pay attention to him and respect him all the time.

"Why? Why should it matter if he's a boy or if he's the oldest?"

I'd always think to myself… I would never tell *Papi*, but I would tell Johnny. My sister, Diana, would tell my parents that it shouldn't matter if he's a boy and she's a girl because they were both responsible, but my parents didn't care. Johnny got to do things that Diana didn't just because he was a boy—like ride farther on his bike, and go to the store by himself and stay home alone, and help *Papi* drive. Girls couldn't do any of those things. Not at our house. We did have to wash the dishes, and sweep and clean the house, and of course cook because only girls did those things. Johnny was the oldest and never had to do any of those things. It wasn't fair. The year was 1968, and the Valley that we now know was very different and so much simpler then. Maybe not fair, but it was simple.

Whether we wanted to or not—we were going to a new city, a big city. We were going to get a new school and new friends, but we weren't sure we wanted that. It was hard to get the things that we wanted. There were five of us kids and only *Papi* worked most of the time so that Mommy could take care of us. But, my sisters and I had figured out early on how to use our baby brother to ask for some things that we wanted.

"Eli, tell *Papi* you want a hamburger."

"*Flechitas, flechitas,*" he'd tell *Papi* in his tiny high-pitched baby voice when we were all cramped up shoulder to shoulder and elbows poking each other crowded in the back seat of our car.

It was always, "Move!"

"You move!"

"How can I move? My back's against the door."

"*¡Yaaa!*"

So...if we were lucky, Eli would stand up in the front seat between Mommy and *Papi*, his tiny little arms stretched out over the front seat bouncing up and down. We loooved it when he would ride in the front. Even though he was small, there would be sooo much more room in the back seat that we were able to move our legs around without fighting or elbowing each other in the stomach. He was still young enough that he would usually listen to us and do what we'd tell him to.

So sometimes, if we were super lucky, *Papi* would stop at the popular teenager's hangout—Whataburger. That of course was the only fast food place in town with the distinctive orange W.

We would always see one of my older cousins, Andy, who used to hang out there with his high school friends. He was one of the very popular guys in high school. All of us would look up to him because he was tall, handsome, and cool like the teens that you would see on TV. Andy and his friends would park their cars on the side of the parking lot up against the orange and white wooden fence and sit on the hoods of them.

As usual we all sat in the car and waited. That's when we saw him. He strutted over to our car, stuck his head in the passenger's window, kissed Mommy on her cheek, and said hello to us while we were anxiously checking to see if we'd see *Papi* come back with our order.

"*Tía* Eliza, hey guys, how's everyone doing?"

"*Te portas bien Andrés, ahorita le voy a hablar a Julia y le voy a decir que te vi con tus amigos y que estaban fumando.*"

"*No, Tía, yo no hago eso*—you know, I'm a Christian! *No te preocupes.* I'm helping them, telling them about Jesus, so they can change their ways."

My *Tía* Julia, my Mommy and the other *tías* would talk on the phone every night without fail, and they would tell each other everything. Mommy had five sisters and four brothers, ten altogether, and they were all very close. For sure Mommy was going to get home, and call my *tía*, and tell her that she saw Andy at Whataburger, and that his friends were smoking. She knew that he was a Christian, but still, she didn't know who the other guys were and that was enough for discussion. They would talk for hours about it. I don't see how they could talk about things like that for so long, but they did. Seeing Andy with his friends and seeing them smoking would surely make my *tía* mad; I just knew it.

Andy started backing away from our car as he saw his friends calling him, the loud base sounds of the music they were listening to blasting in the parking lot.

He yelled out a "¡Hey, *Tío* Juan!"

By then, *Papi* was coming back with our burgers and a gallon of root beer in a glass gallon container along with a bag of Fritos. Every so often we would be treated to that special delicacy. My dad would buy us one Whataburger cut up, and we would each get a slice of it. It was the best. Slowly we'd pull out of the Whataburger driveway with all of our heads sticking out of the back windows waving to Andy as the thundering sound of *The Beatles*, "Revolution," faded away.

"Bye, Andy! Bye!" We'd all be yelling at him. I wonder if he was as excited to see us.

"We forgot to tell him the news!" Johnny yelled out.

"Go back…so we can tell him that we're moving."

"Don't worry." Mommy tells us. "*Ahorita le hablo a Julia.*"

The Hurricane

Just months before 1968, the Rio Grande Valley experienced a historic, catastrophic hurricane that took everyone by surprise. Hurricane Beulah swept into South Texas destroying and flooding many homes and businesses.

That day the winds were getting strong, and we were playing outside spinning and spinning until we would fall down. Our neighbor Lina ran over across the empty lot through the little trail that we had made from going back and forth to each other's houses over and over again to tell Mommy that they were leaving to the shelter.

"Se cuidan, Eliza—me avisas cuando regresen."

"Mommy, everyone is leaving…what about us?"

"We have to wait for your father," Mommy said as she rushed back and forth quickly packing for our temporary trip.

Papi had gone to *Amá* Magda's to make sure our grandparents were going to come with us to our shelter. He didn't want them to stay behind, especially not for this storm. Leaves and branches were flying by us and the sky was getting dark grey. Outside, the neighbors' windows were boarded and taped up. None of the kids were playing except us.

"Everyone's gone! What if the storm comes and we can't leave?" Johnny looks at me.

"Then, our house will spin up into the sky and take us with it, and who knows where we'll land."

"What, What do you mean?"

"Well, we may end up in some far off, strange place, if at all."

"Oh no! What's going to happen to us?" As I'm about to run crying to Mommy, *Papi* arrives telling us we need to leave because the hurricane was coming.

As we started to get into the car, I stopped. "No! We can't… What about Lobo?" He was nowhere.

"He'll be fine," *Papi* said. "Don't worry; dogs can take care of themselves. Besides, he's a wolf."

I didn't want to leave him, but we could never go against my *Papi* because what he said was just how it was, so I worried about him and hoped that he would be fine. We quickly loaded up Mommy's food and clothes that she packed for us, and we left.

When we arrived at the shelter, we were bubbling with excitement. We were at the school where *Papi* was the principal, and we were actually going to stay in the teacher's lounge. Kids were never allowed; it was off limits, but now we were all getting to see the actual inside of the teachers' sacred room.

There was a Coke machine, a coffee pot, a sink, sofas, a table, a bathroom, and even a TV; it was just like a house, except a different house. The best part was that *Amá* Magda, *Apá* Juan, Cheta, Fita, Beto, and Lori were with us. It was like a sleepover party; we had blankets, games, cards, and food—it was going to be so much fun.

During our stay my grandma would make us all sandwiches out of Deviled Ham with the little red devil on the white paper packaging and Potted Meat, and we would play cards to pass the time.

"I hate those devil sandwiches."

"For now, that's what we have," Mommy would tell me. "When this is over I'll make all of you some *caldo*." After a while we started to get tired of the teacher's lounge.

"Can we walk to the girls' bathroom outside? We'll all go together."

Usually we wouldn't be allowed, but we were so many, and the lounge only had one bathroom so, *Papi* let Lori, Diana and I go out to the schools' hallway restrooms during the storm. It was such an adventure for us. He wouldn't have let us go, but the bathrooms were just a few doors down from us, and Lori was going with us. *Papi* trusted her to take care of us. All of us were holding hands as we proceeded out the door with Mommy watching us as we stepped out. "¡*Cuidado*!" She yelled.

"Don't worry Eliza."

Lori was the same age as Johnny. She was my aunt, but she never seemed like an aunt to me; she was just one of us. It was always hard for me to imagine that Mommy and *Amá* Magda were pregnant at the same time, but Johnny and Lori were both born in May only a few weeks apart. How can she be my aunt if she's our age? It never made sense to me, but that's how it was. The winds were unbearably strong that we had to hold onto the red and blue painted poles on the side of the hallway. My tiny body would get tossed by the forceful winds like a ragdoll in a mad dog's mouth, and then I'd run and grab the other pole until we finally made it to the girl's bathroom.

"Wow!"

"How are we going to make it back?"

"It's not that far."

"Maybe we should wait."

"We shouldn't have come."

"Stop crying." Diana scolded me. "We can do it."

My sister was always the most positive and would always find a way to get things done. Holding hands, we started back, jumping from red pole to blue pole trying to hug them with both arms tightly. We'd let go and get thrown by the fierce winds only to get grabbed by each other's hand. We could see Mommy worriedly standing at the door of the teacher's lounge with the—I knew it look. Bravely we made it back to our base as Mommy, *Amá* Magda, Cheta, and Fita wrapped us up in towels.

"*¡Qué bárbaras!*" All of them told us as they dried us off.

"*¿Tienen hambre m'ijitas, pobrecitas?*" *Amá* Magda asked, as she took out the loaf of bread and Deviled Ham.

"I'm starving!" Johnny said. Of course, he would be.

After two days at our shelter, *Papi* said that we could finally go home, if the storm passed. He stepped outside to make sure.

"*Ahora sí, ¡vámonos!*"

"¡Yay!" We were all so excited.

My cocoon. I wanted to get back to our own bed that the three of us shared even if we'd kick each other and fight for the pillows. It was our home, not a shelter, not a teacher's lounge. The school had been fun at first, but after a while it was boring because we weren't allowed to go outside. The slumber party ended up lasting much longer than we thought. Our imagination only took us so far before a fight broke out that had to be refereed by one of my *tías*. There was a TV in the teacher's lounge, with channel four and five, just like the one we had at home, but it only worked for a little while on the first day and then suddenly stopped working even though we tried putting foil on the rabbit ear antennas. It still wouldn't work.

"Johnny, move it to the right, no pick it up higher. There. No—nothing…"

"*¡Chihuahuas*! *Haber*! Let me do it!" *Tía* Cheta, going for the bent ear would say.

"We need to watch the news! How are we supposed to know what's going on *hombre*?" We were all out of luck because all the electricity was out. What made things bad was that we were also running out of food and even though I hated Deviled Ham, it was better than nothing.

Mommy, *Amá* Magda, Cheta, and Fita had started packing up blankets and all of the stuff that they had brought. They were scrubbing and cleaning every little corner of that lounge. The storm had passed; we would finally get to go outside. Anxiously, we crammed out of the door onto the flooded hallways.

"You go first."

"No, you go; you're the one that was pushing me out of the way." I moved to the side and let Diana get by, since she was older and more responsible. There was water everywhere and tree branches were scattered all over the place.

"All of you help take these boxes to the car."

Papi needed our help so we all grabbed a box and followed him out to the flooded parking lot to pack up our car. My grandparents and aunts did the same with their stuff, and Mommy tried her best to continue cleaning up the lounge in every nook and cranny. One by one we filed into our car cramped with all of the extra stuff and elbows on our tummies, but we knew it would be a short ride home. *Papi* was nervous to see if our house had made it through the storm, as were our grandparents with their home. We quickly said our goodbyes out in the flooded parking lot to *Amá* Magda and *Apá* Juan bowing our heads waiting for her *bendición*. *Amá* Magda never left us without her blessing.

"*En el nombre Del Padre, El Hijo, Y El Espíritu Santo,*" she told us as she made the sign of the cross on each of our heads telling us goodbye. After that we had protection. We then waved out of the windows of our car. Our heads sticking out catching the wind and trying to get wet with the water that was splashing onto the car from the flooded streets we were passing.

"Go faster! Go faster! ¡Ándale Papi!"

We hoped *Papi* would make our car go super-fast so that the water would splash in our vehicle and get us all wet. My parents were too busy looking out of their front windows at homes with roofs torn off, store signs broken in pieces, electrical wires dangling from poles, and trees placed strategically in the middle of the road.

Suddenly, I remembered. "What about Lobo? My Lobo." Crying, I was scared to get to our house because there was no way he could have made it through this hurricane.

"We need to worry about our house." *Papi* said, "Dogs can take care of themselves. How can you be worrying about Lobo right now when we don't even know if our house will be there when we get back?"

I put my head down into my hands feeling bad that I was thinking about my dog instead of our house, but I couldn't help it; that's how I felt. I was hoping Lobo was okay; what if something terrible had happened to him? Slowly we approached our neighborhood. It looked like an ocean with broken houses and trees around it.

"Can we go swimming? Please?"

Whenever it rained and the streets flooded we got to

swim in our instant swimming pool along with the entire neighborhood kids. Except this time, Mommy and *Papi* didn't seem as if they wanted us to swim. We didn't see any of our friends swimming either. As we approached our house, the trees in front that we climbed had fallen onto the street, but our house looked normal. *Papi* sighed, parked the car in its usual spot, and all of us jumped out—Johnny, Diana, Keki, Eli, and me. We started to splash onto the water-filled pool before anyone could stop us.

"Lobo! Lobo!"

I started calling, but I couldn't find him anywhere. Everyone started to help me look for him all around the house. "Oh, please God let my Lobo be safe." I closed my eyes in prayer as I formed the sign of the cross on my forehead, chest, then left and right shoulder finishing it off with a kiss on my hand. I began to think that maybe my puppy was gone, when out from under the house popped his little wolf head.

"Lobo! My Lobo!"

I tried to swoop him up in my arms, but could not lift him.

"You were right *Papi*; he did hide under the house!"

Sure enough, just like *Papi* had said he would be, he was safe. He was perfect and very excited to see all of us. Jumping and jumping on us, he nearly knocked me to the ground. What a true wolf! If only they would have allowed dogs at the school.

"I told you he'd be fine, now let's get busy."

We started to get everything back inside the house. We still didn't have water or electricity because of the storm, but we were home, and Lobo was home. The hurricane was over.

The Lesbian

Picking up my teenage sons after school that day was extra hectic.

"Hey, Mom! Where are you going? What's up? Whoa—Why all dressed up?"

As always, they were all talking to me at once. Joshua, Mark, and David all attended high school in a city thirty minutes away from our home, so they rode a bus to their home school where I picked them up. Being the mom of four sons, my world was surrounded by boys. Rigo, my oldest was away at college. Joshua and Mark, my teens were complete opposites, and Paul, the baby was only in sixth grade. They were all two years apart, plus this year our German exchange student, David, lived with us. I could handle hectic days, but today I was nervous, and they could tell. Rigo, the leader of the group had graduated from the same school the previous year and was now away at D.C., Paul, their younger brother, unfortunately dealt with all of them telling him what to do all of the time, was still in elementary school.

David had arrived unexpectedly from Germany and needed a host family, so we gladly took the job when his original host family backed out. Actually, Mr. Davis, the high school sponsor for the exchange program called me.

"Suzy, I need your help. David's host family can't take him after all, and he needs a family. Talk to Bert and come over to the school to fill out the paperwork."

There was no need to talk about it; we knew that we would take David in. That afternoon my husband and I drove to the high school, filled out the millions of papers, and signed our lives away to be responsible for David.

"I'll take him over to y'all's house tomorrow, thanks guys."

Daniel Davis had been a family friend for years. He was all three of our older boys' teacher. Rigo had been to Germany with his school group and now Mark was going to be going this year. We had hosted two other German students before, but only for a one-month stay. Now, David would be living with us for the entire year. The more the merrier.

"Hurry up guys! We still have to go get Paul!"

They threw their backpacks in the last seat of our SUV and clicked the seatbelts on while Joshua cranked on the XM radio.

"I got y'all some gators."

"Thanks mom, but I was hoping we could go for *raspas*."

Not that I spoiled them, but they loved going for a *raspa* after school. In 100 degrees nothing tasted better than to have that soft flavored ice melting in your mouth to cool you off. It was their favorite treat, and even David had gotten addicted to them.

"We have no such thing in Germany," he'd say.

"Sorry, Baby not today."

"That's fine, Mom. So—where you going?" Joshua gulps his drink asking nonchalantly.

"Look boys." I turn the knob on the radio down.

"Remember Daniela? I've told you about her, my childhood best friend, so many times before. She lived down the street when I was growing up?"

Uninterested they keep drinking their gators and looking out the window as we pass some of their friends by, and they wave and nod their head in acknowledgment at some of the kids.

"Daniela—my childhood friend!"

I continue even though they don't seem to remember or care. Then all of a sudden Mark wakes up and yells out making me and everyone else in the car turnaround in surprise.

"Oh yeah! The lesbian, right?"

Then, as if they're all waking up from a trance, they all start paying attention.

"Who's that?" David asks?

We all feel sorry for David because without warning he's come into our lives and thrown into our Mexican American culture with so many relatives and traditions spun into his regular academic curriculum. He didn't ask for us; he just got us. We didn't ask for him either; we just ended up with him literally on our doorstep. The English must be hard for him to keep straight, but then he keeps hearing Spanish and Tex-Mex everywhere we go. It seems as if there are always new people for him to meet as well.

"So who is Daniela the lesbian, a relative?" David asks again in his German accent. "Have I met her?"

"Oh, that Daniela!"

Joshua suddenly remembers as we arrive at Paul's school, and he jumps into the back seat over Mark and David joining in the conversation.

"Hey, watch it! That's my foot you landed on Baby!

Mom's telling us about her best friend, Daniela, the lesbian."

"This is so cool! Your mom's best friend is a lesbian."

David of course chimes in and loves the idea of her being a lesbian.

"In Germany, everyone is accepting, but I'm not sure about here."

"No, she wasn't always a lesbian. We grew up together, were super close, best friends. I would practically live at her house, but things changed for us in high school. We grew apart and sort of went our separate ways. She ended up getting pregnant and eloped with her boyfriend her senior year. That seemed to happen with many of my friends that year. It wasn't until her daughter grew up that she realized she was a lesbian; I've told you guys all this a million times before. I haven't seen her in years, but we were best friends when we were kids, inseparable."

"Mom, you can't become gay. She was born that way but probably didn't know it. You know, like the song. Being gay isn't a choice—you know that." They all lecture me.

"All I know is that we were always best friends, since we were babies. She lived down the street, and we did everything together. In high school she got pregnant and had to get married because that's what girls did back then. It was the right thing to do. She had an adorable baby girl named Daphne. After Daphne grew up she got divorced and then realized she was a lesbian. She'll always be my childhood best friend though."

"Mom, she was always a lesbian!"

"Anyway, listen boys; it doesn't matter. What does matter is that her mom has passed away, and I have to see her. I'm going to get y'all home right now unless you'd instead go with me."

"I'm sure she'd love to meet you guys."

They look at each other and shake their heads as if saying no way, not me.

"Then please no fighting; your dad will be home later. Dinner is ready on the stove. I have to go to Weslaco right now to see Daniela at the funeral home as much as I hate those God-awful places. I found out today, and you know how your dad and I have always told you how important it is to see the family after someone you care about has died. I have to go."

The boys all hug me and tell me that they're sorry about my friend's mom as they jump off of the car and slam the door. "Bye, Mom! Love you!"

I drive off into the road of unknown as if I'm a cast member of the *Twilight Zone*. Cars passing me, yet not knowing that they are there. I am catapulted into a time that existed years ago…

Ever since the first grade my best friend was Daniela, and she was always a bit rough, but she and her sister had everything. The best part was that they had the entire Barbie collection. They not only had the dolls, but all of the clothes, cars, houses, and accessories. They also had an organ at her home in their living room that I would get to play. I loved to ride my purple banana seat bike to the end of the street all of the time. Daniela lived in the only brick house in our neighborhood, on the corner, at the opposite end of our street with her parents Mina, Yneo, and her sister Elvira, who looked like a child movie star and nothing like Daniela. Everyone said that they were adopted that's why they didn't look alike, but I never knew for sure nor did I care. When we were in first grade, one of my friends invited me to her birthday party.

Daniela came up to me looking at the invitation in my hand.

"You're not going to that, are you?"

"I want to go, she's my friend."

"No, if you go then you won't be my best friend anymore."

How could I lose my best friend? I took the invitation and threw it in the trash because it just wasn't worth making Daniela mad. She was happy about that. After school, we would walk home together. Hand in hand, we would cross through the park and stop to play on the swings pushing each other. Running across the play area we'd land on the merry go round and push each other on that until we got so tired. Finally, we'd continue on our journey and make another stop at the hospital to drink water from the water fountains inside. Then, we'd walk through the main lobby and out the emergency room entrance because it was a shortcut. When we'd come out the door, Daniela's house would be across the street. She'd go home, and I'd make a run for it as if I had to win a race through the alley so that the neighborhood dogs wouldn't chase me. There were tons of mean dogs where we lived, but I knew just how to sneak past them and then outrun them.

Finally, safe and sound at home Mommy would welcome me with "*¿Tienes hambre*? How was school?" That of course was the best part of all.

I didn't have a party for my seventh birthday. I didn't have friends over. I did get a purple banana seat bike with a basket on the handlebars. That was the absolute best bike ever. Daniela, my best friend and I would ride all over the neighborhood on our bikes as if we were riding motorcycles through a big city. The feel of the wind blowing against our face and our hair aimlessly flying by was amazing. No need for shoes either, we were free spirits and both big show-offs. Before long, I learned different tricks on my bike.

"Look, Daniela I can ride with no hands!" I would ride for a few seconds, and then I'd grab the handlebar.

"Me too!" Daniela would copy me.

We would do this over and over until we both got pretty good at no hands.

"I can ride up the entire block without hands." Daniela thought she was better than me.

"Let's race! No hands!" I challenged her to a friendly competition. "From my house to yours. Ready. GO!"

We were off riding down the street with the dogs barking and chasing us, but they couldn't catch us. Laughing with the dogs chasing after us we would forget about the race and park our bikes at Daniela's house for a break.

"Let's play Barbies!"

Running inside the back door past Mina who was busy in the kitchen we'd hurl ourselves into our little cave, Daniela's bedroom, and escape into a make-believe world. Without realizing it, hours had passed, and it was time for me to go home.

"See you tomorrow!"

Grabbing my motorcycle and putting it into gear, I was off into the sunset.

"*¿Dónde estabas?*"

"Mommy, I was at Daniela's. We were playing."

"*¡Ay, qué niña está!*"

Morning couldn't come fast enough.

"I'll be at Daniela's," I yelled out as I grabbed my banana seat purple bicycle.

Wearing my purple shorts and matching shirt, I felt powerful as I stood on the pedals with my bare feet pedaling feeling the wind on me and making my shirt fly like a kite. I'd wave my hands up in the air as if I was riding a roller coaster with the brush of strong winds against my body.

Suddenly, in the corner of my eye I caught a glimpse of him. It was one of our neighbors, and he was playing out in his yard. Yes, it was Jaime. Two houses down from us, he was the youngest in his family and very popular. He was the cutest boy in our neighborhood, so I had to show off in front of him.

"Hi, Jaime!" I yelled out. "Look, I can ride my bike with no hands and no feet!"

I picked up my hands super high in the air and picked up my feet as well while I looked over at Jaime with a great big goofy smile.

"Oh, hi! Yeah, that's great—I guess."

He didn't even care. As I turned to grab the handlebars and pedals, it happened. I don't know how it happened, but it did. CRASH! I fell off by beautiful bike while my foot got tangled in the chain. There I was lying on the street in a pool of blood and my foot stuck in my bike's chain. Weird though…I didn't feel anything. I took my foot and yanked it out of the chain, got back up on my banana seat and pedaled as fast as I could to Daniela's house because I knew she was waiting for me. Sure enough she was waiting for me outside.

"What happened to you?"

She cried out as she ran for the garden hose turning it on full force and spraying it on my foot to wash away the blood.

"Noooooo! Don't do that! What's the matter with you?"

As she sprayed my wound, we saw how deep the cut was, which exposed the bone on my foot.

"I don't feel anything." I told Daniela—"How weird, huh?"

"You stay here; I need to go call your mom on the phone."

Blood was rapidly gushing while Mommy arrived and wrapped my cut up quickly. She put me in the back seat of the car and drove me to the emergency room. I got twelve stitches on my foot. The doctor said that my bone had been chipped. The best part was Mommy took me to Whataburger afterward and got me a vanilla shake, and my brothers and sisters were all jealous because they didn't get one.

That was so long ago and now I'm standing facing a coffin with my best friend's mom laying peacefully with a *Rosario* wrapped around her hands.

"I knew you would come," the voice behind me says as I turn around.

"Oh, Daniela I'm so sorry about your mommy!"

She grabs my hand and sits me down next to her as we both face the white box. With my arm around her, tears flow out of her eyes and dribble down her face splashing on my hand.

"Who's this?" An irate voice says as I quickly turn to see someone I had never seen before.

"Babe, this is my forever best friend. Remember I told you about her."

"I'm Daniela's girlfriend." She gave me a look and sat in the chair on Daniela's other side.

"I'm so sorry about your loss." I acknowledge her, and Daniela, and I continue talking as she continues to give me a look.

"Don't worry; we're just friends. That's it, really."

50

As I get up to leave, she quickly stands and sits in the chair that I was sitting in placing her arm around her girlfriend. I turn around and smile at them.

"Thanks," Daniela mouths as I wave at her and walk out the door.

Mrs. Sells

The summer after first grade quickly passed us by and soon we all returned to Louise Black School eager to get back to our regular routines. I was excited to go back to school to see all of my friends and to see my teacher from the previous year. She had been such a great teacher; she was just like a mom while we were at school. During Easter she had taken the entire class to her house for an Easter Egg Hunt and a picnic. Mrs. Sells was like a second mom to all of her students and took care of all of us. She was beautiful with her blonde hair that curled up and flipped up on her shoulder. Her glasses, pointed on the edges with rhinestones, made her look like a model from *Vogue* magazine. Oh, I admired her so much. All of the kids in her class thought that they were lucky because she was their teacher. Not only was she pretty, but she was so nice to all of us and treated us like her children. We felt special around her; we were special around her. The kids in the other classes were all jealous of us because we had the best first-grade teacher. Even though we started school speaking Spanish, she didn't mind. She helped us with English, and all of us in her class were way ahead of the other classes.

Now that we were in second grade, all of my classmates were in a class with a different teacher, and none of us had seen Mrs. Sells. During recess we were all wondering where she was.

"I saw Cindy, her daughter, in the hall." Pablo said to all of us.

Pablo was our leader. He would organize us during recess and have our group rehearse plays that he would think of, and then we would perform them in front of our class. Our group had about six kids in it, two boys and four girls including myself. We would always meet at the irrigation ditch right next to the street in the playground during recess. The ditch was our secret place because we could speak all of the Spanish that we wanted, and we wouldn't get in trouble because the teachers couldn't hear us out there.

Whatever Pablo said we believed for some reason, and we would do what he would tell us.

"You know that Cindy is a sixth grader, right?"

Pablo continued with his story about Cindy. We were all listening because we wanted to know why Cindy was here and not Mrs. Sells.

"Did you ask her about her mom?" Lila asked.

"No, I couldn't ask her that."

Lila and Pablo were best friends and always together. I thought it was strange that he couldn't ask.

"Why not, why couldn't you ask? You know we all want to know where she is. Why couldn't you ask her?"

He looked at me straight in my eyes and said,

"Listen, I know you guys don't want to hear this, but something terrible happened during the summer. My big brother told me that he heard Cindy's friends talking about her."

We looked at him with big question marks on our faces. "What are you talking about? What happened to her?"

He just shook his head back and forth looking down and quietly said with a sigh — "She died."

 Our eyes popped wide open like huge golf balls.

"She what?"

"*¡Se murió!*"

He then translated in Spanish as if that would make us understand better. Just like that, Pablo was telling my friends and me that our teacher was dead.

"What! What are you talking about? She can't be dead. I don't believe you. Is this one of your jokes?"

"*¡De verdad! No estoy jugando!*"

He was always playing weird jokes and pranks on us and making all of us laugh, and I thought this was one of those because it just didn't make any sense. I surely didn't know anyone who had died before. Our teacher could not have been one of the people to die; it could not be possible. I had been to her house and played in her yard. She lived by the water with the cute ducks and lots of green grass all around her house. It looked like it came out of one of the picture books she used to read to us after lunch, when we'd all gather around her. She would read in her soft-spoken voice, and we would all struggle to see the pretty pictures that she would be holding up to show us. Mrs. Sells was so lovely, the perfect teacher; she reminded me of Mommy.

"Go ahead and find out for yourself then. I dare you." Pablo was daring me.

"What are you talking about?" I looked at him knowing that he was up to something. He returned the look.

"I dare you to ask Cindy what happened to her mom." Then everyone else went along and chimed in with Pablo.

"We all dare you. Ask Cindy."

54

We were all second graders in an elementary school with first through sixth graders, and Cindy was a sixth grader. Second graders usually didn't go and mingle with the sixth graders, but this was a dare. They had their own hall, and only sixth graders were allowed to walk through there.

"Are you chicken?" They all started.

"Chicken! Chicken! Chicken!"

I couldn't stand it. I also couldn't stand my friends calling me chicken.

"Fine, I'll go and ask her; it's not true anyway—nothing to lose, right? I know it's not true. I'll ask her. I'll ask her at lunch."

We went back to class, and I couldn't get used to our new teacher. All I could do was think if it could be true about Mrs. Sells. How could she have died? It's not true. I will not believe it. The only thing I could do was to wait for lunch, look for Cindy, and ask her. Then I would know that it was all a lie.

As the bell rang, I didn't even grab my brown lunch-bag to join my friends. I ran out to the hall and started walking to the sixth-grade hall where all of the older kids hung out at lunchtime. My brother was in the sixth grade, so I bumped into him as I passed him in the hall with his friends.

"What are you doing over here? Only the big kids are allowed on this side of the school."

He looked at me squinting his eyes and twitching his nose.

"I'm doing something for my teacher," I told him.

If I had said anything then he would have told Mommy, and I would have gotten in trouble. I had to lie; I had no choice. Finally, he left me alone, and I went on to the forbidden hall to look for Cindy.

The next hall was the sixth-grade hall. As I approached it, I saw her sitting with a group of other big kids. I took a deep breath. She didn't know who I was. Nor had I ever spoken to her either. All of us in her moms' class knew her because Mrs. Sells had pictures of her family on her desk. We had all seen her in school and thought that she looked so much like her mom. She was probably just as smart too since Mrs. Sells was her mom. Not being discouraged, I slowly went up to her from behind and tapped her shoulder. She turned around and looked at me.

"Hi!" She tells me as I take a deep breath and blurt out my words.

"Is it true that your mother died?"

She just looked at me in disbelief and burst into tears, jumped up and ran away. Her friends looked at me with mad faces as they all started towards me.

"How could you do that? That is so mean of you?"

I had no idea what they were talking about, so I just walked away and went back to my classroom. I waited for the bell to ring. My friends came running in and wanted to know what happened because they heard that Cindy had gone home crying.

"Did you ask her?"

I said nothing. I was still in shock that it was true and that no one had told me. No one had ever told me how to deal with this before. It had never happened before. Just then Mrs. Sanders came into our room. She was our new teacher and didn't look at all like Mrs. Sells. There was a feeling that she seemed to have about her.

"Class, I need to talk to all of you about something that happened during lunch."

I just knew what she was going to say and it was going to be about me. "Here we go with the lecture," I thought as the shivers began to spread throughout my body.

"Sometimes during our life, we will lose those who we love dearly, and we don't know how to express those feelings. We realize that many of you cared very much for Mrs. Sells and were unaware of her passing. She was like a mother to many of you, and we are very sorry for your loss. If you need to talk about this you can talk to one of our counselors or to me, but her family is still too emotional to deal with it, so please don't try to talk to any of them about her right now."

That was it. She didn't mention my name. She didn't get mad at me. She said it all with a smile. After the bell rang for the end of school I went up to Mrs. Sander's desk. I hugged her and thanked her for being so nice.

Looking up at her face that was much older than Mrs. Sells', I swallow and say, "It was me," as she looks down at me.

"I know it was you, sweetie. She meant a lot to you, I know. There's no way that I can replace her. She'll always have a special place in your heart, but I'll always be here for you if you need anything." I hugged her again tighter this time and said goodbye.

L*a Bendición*

Before the big move to Houston, *Papi* bought a brand-new car. It wasn't a new used car like the ones that we had before; it was an amazing, shiny, light yellow, four-door, Ford, with air conditioning. Wow! We were doing better now. It was a step up from the navy-blue Batmobile we had before. There was no way that our old car would have made the long haul to the big city, and the many trips back to the Valley to visit, so the investment was a must. Thus, he and Mommy put all five of us kids in the back seat of our American made Ford, and did what everyone did in those days when they bought a new car (at least in our family); he took us to *Amá* Magda's house to show her and *Apá* Juan (our grandparents) the new car. We were all bouncing up and down in the back as we approached the familiar *barrio*. Their small, faded, light pink frame home stood out in the neighborhood for some reason, with its bits of paint peeling off, on Texas Avenue. It was still decorated with political signs left from the previous primaries because every single election was an integral part of our lives in the Santos family. The God-given right to vote and do our part as American citizens for our country was instilled in us at an early age. My father's side of the family had always been political and democratic as any United States family could be. Not only was the outside of their home peppered with election signs, but inside you could always find picket signs ready to go for protests and buttons to be handed out on the kitchen table right next to the plate of freshly made *tortillas* and pot of hot coffee. Politics was always a subject discussed at my grandparents' home. Elections were always crucial, and the entire family always worked those big days.

Finally, we were at my grandmother's and excitement consumed us. First, *Amá* Magda, came out dressed as always in her dark navy-blue dress right above her ankles with her flat black shoes. I never saw my grandma wear anything other than dark colors. *Papi* had told us that it was because she was always in mourning. When he was twelve years old his little two-year-old brother died. The people that they worked for up north refused to take them to town to get help for him, and they didn't have their transportation. They made them wait until it was too late. His baby brother had a high fever that would not go down. *Amá* Magda had begged to be taken to the doctor, but the owners of the farm that they were working refused to take anyone into town until everyone would go on Saturday. Saturdays were a big day for the migrants. They would all go to town together and buy whatever they needed. This time though, it was an emergency, and they had no way to get to town. When they finally convinced someone to drive them—*Papi*'s baby brother died. Since *Papi* was the oldest son, he had to take care of all of the funeral arrangements while *Apá* Juan worked. *Papi* was the only one who could speak and write in English, so he had to walk to town, sign the death certificate, pick out a coffin, and burial site, and all else that had to be done when a loved one dies. *Papi* was only twelve.

Her hair was braided and rolled up in a neat bun on the back of her head. (I remember watching her comb and braid her hair when we would stay at her house surprised at how long it was.) Alongside of her was *Apá* Juan in his khaki pants and work shirt, chiseled face and almost stoic expression; he always had such a dry sense of humor that I didn't understand until I was much older. Behind them were my *tías* Cheta and Fita, two of a kind, yet such opposites. Both lived with my grandparents, never married and were all of the cousins' favorites. All of us stepped out of the car so that they could sit inside and examine it to give their approval. After they did, my grandma, *Amá* Magda, stepped out in front of it, lifted her right hand, and gave her *bendición*.

"*En el nombre Del Padre, Del Hijo, y Del Espíritu Santo,*" (blessed it while forming the sign of the cross with her hands) and did the same to us as we crawled back inside.

Every time that we would visit *Amá* Magda's house, we could not leave without her giving us her special *bendición*. It became a ritual that she did for us until the day she died, and is something that I miss about her so very much.

We loved going there because my aunts would spoil all of their nieces and nephews. Her house was quite interesting and so much fun for all of the cousins. There was the main house, which was a small frame home with a broken sidewalk leading up to a cement porch that was connected to a carport that always had a car in it that my aunt always seemed to be working on. Many times when we'd get there, my *Tía* Cheta would be busy messing with a car and all you would be able to see would be her legs. Everyone would go inside, but I liked staying outside with my aunt and asking her what she was doing.

"You see this?" Pulling out the oil stick and wiping it down with a rag she continued.

"You wipe it and then stick it back in again. Then you measure how much oil the car has. It tells you right here if you need to add more. You see?"

"Wow! So then you need to add some?" I noticed that it was pretty low on oil.

"Yup, I figured I did; that's why I'm checking it. I can do this myself. There's no need to take it to someone else to do it for me. When you start driving, don't ever take your car to anyone to do this, you hear me. You can do this stuff yourself. It's easy."

She looked me right in my eye holding her oily stick and pointing it at me.

"*¿Entiendes? Tienes que aprender.*"

"Thanks, *Tía* Cheta! I'll always remember how to do this."

She then grabbed a can of oil and put it in. Then she proceeded to grab a small towel.

"You need to be careful when opening this here because it's usually hot. This is where the water goes. Always make sure that your car has enough water in it." She then turned the hot gasket and opened it up as steam poured out of it.

"See, I told you so. Now grab that water hose down there." I got the water hose and gave it to her.

"You do it; pour the water in that opening there. I'll tell you when to stop." I felt so important because I was helping my aunt with her car.

"Okay, stop. That's all you need. You see, it's that simple. Now, look at these things over here. These are the spark plugs."

She just kept on and on telling me all about the car and the engine, the battery and how to charge it.

"How do you know all this?" I'd ask her.

"*Mira m'ijita*; I pay attention, listen, and watch. Not just everything that you learn in school is what counts; you're learning all the time. It's all-important. It doesn't matter if it's a car or a sink; if it breaks you need to know how to fix it."

I was so impressed with her because there were so many things that she knew how to do. She could fix anything, and no one had taught her how to do it.

Political signs always decorated their small front yard; it looked like a polling site for an election except during the Christmas holidays when it was completely decked out with a million lights, and then it looked like a Las Vegas Casino. My other *Tía* Fita was responsible for that, and she took great pride in it as well. She had reason to feel proud; she would win the annual Christmas house-decorating contest every year. A year would not go by without her outdoing what she did the previous year. Lines of cars would pile up in the *barrio* to see the 1st prizewinner—my grandmother's house.

"Eliza, I have a great idea for this year's Christmas contest. Bring the kids in their choir robes this afternoon. The judges are coming about six p.m., so make sure that they're here about five."

My *Tía* Fita frantically called Mommy asking her to make sure we were at my grandmother's house that afternoon. We had no clue what was going on, but we did what we were told.

When we arrived at *Amá* Magda's house, my other cousins who were in the church choir with us were also there.

"*Miren*, this is very important! I need for all of you to stand out in front by the street and sing Christmas songs as loud as you can. I'll let you know when you can stop."

We all looked at each other confused. It was Keki, Alda, Avelina, Nacho, Mireya, Mati, and myself all standing on my grandmother's porch.

"What? You mean we're living props? Nacho said." *Tía* Fita anxiously looked at him and kept glancing out at the street that was already busy with traffic.

"No, I need help because this year the competition is very tough. If I don't do something different—I'll lose. All of you know how much this means to me."

She worked on this all year making the decorations by hand and making sure that all of the lights worked. Most of the time the lights needed to be restrung, and she would do whatever she needed to do to not buy new ones.

"We'll do it!" All of us said as we started to walk out to the lot.

It was the least we could do. As we walked, we started singing *"Oh Holy Night…"*

By the end of the song, nightfall began to creep up on us and the cars were streaming by. Kids and adults alike were hanging out of windows to catch a glimpse of us.

"I think we're a hit." Alda said to me before we started our next carol.

"We're an overnight sensation." I said as we all started laughing.

We looked over to my aunt who was standing under the edge of the porch discreetly, and she gave us a sign to keep singing. Continuing, we then sang, *Rocking Around the Christmas Tree and Feliz Navidad.* She was happy.

After the songs, *Tía* Fita came running up to us so excited that she couldn't refrain from hugging all of us.

"You did it; if I win it will be all because of you guys. You can relax now because the judges just left." All of us took a deep breath.

"Yay! Now we can change and go inside."

We did like singing, but it would be more fun to go in and play a board game or something since we were all there.

"¡*Espérense*! I said the judges passed, but look at all of the cars. They want to see you guys, and they want to hear all of you sing. You can't leave."

"What? We didn't even know we were going to do this."

All of us looked at each other and then at my aunt who seemed so disappointed.

"Well...it is Christmastime. We really should be doing for others. Fine *Tía*, we'll do it. Next year though, please don't have any live props." We all started to head back to our spot by the street as passersby yelled and honked their horns at us.

"You see, they love you."

In the lot to the right were four small frame apartments that were always rented out to different interesting tenants that would come and go. Behind the house, was the *cuartito* full of boxes and stuff that we loved going through. When my *tías* or *Amá* Magda took us in there it was magical because we could find almost anything. Whenever we needed special clothes or items for projects, we'd get them from that *cuartito*.

On the opposite side of the house was the best part— *Amá* Magda had a *tiendita* for the *barrio,* and she would let us get whatever we wanted every time we went over. My *Tía* Cheta would also allow us to run the cash register with her.

"Get over here; you see this button? When you need to open the register press it, and it opens up. Over here is the notepad where we keep everyone's record."

Next to the old cash register was a record book with names of everyone in the neighborhood, dates, and amounts of items purchased with IOU's.

"If one of the neighbors comes in and wants to buy something but doesn't have money because they haven't been paid yet; they ask us to just *apúntalo*."

"I can handle it."

We would feel so important if we got to sit at the register and wait on customers. The neighbors would come in and buy bread, milk, or sodas. We would add it up and get the notebook out most of the time.

Sometimes my grandmother had a special treat for us. The *hielero* would come and drop off a huge block of ice for her. She had an icebox that she kept in the front of the store. When she made *raspas*, everyone in the neighborhood knew and would gather all around her. Of course we would always get the first ones. *Amá* Magda would make the syrups herself in her kitchen, and the taste was as sweet as candy. The scraper she used to shave the ice from the big chunk was huge, and she would maneuver it with such preciseness and delicateness that the *raspas* came out as soft as snow. No one else could make *raspas* like my grandmother. She would pack on the ice in a small mountain and then pour the special recipe that only she knew how to make over it. Yummmm! It was so good. The line of neighbors would stretch out along the street waiting to get their delicious snack, and word would spread quickly in the *barrio*. As fast as the iceman would deliver the block of ice, the *raspas* would disappear.

"*Que Dios los bendiga,*" you could always hear her say as she made a motion with her hands of the sign of the cross.

L os Torritos

Mama Jesusa's house was a tiny frame house with one small room in the back of it, but that didn't stop her and my grandfather, *Apá* Maximiliano, from taking people in. From time to time various people lived at my grandparent's home. Some were going through a difficult time, and others just needed a place to stay for a while, but they would always take them in. One of these men was Cowboy.

We'd arrive at *Mama* Jesusa's house full of excitement knowing that there would always be cousins there to play with. When you have such a large family as we do, it would never fail that my grandparents were never alone. As we drove up Los Torritos Street, we could see him sitting on the steps with his big hat. He was very tall and had red sunburned skin. His hands were calloused, and he would sit on the steps with his arms crossed, chewing on something. He always had on worn, scuffed, pointy cowboy boots with a western shirt that had the shiny buttons. His blue jeans were also worn from some mysterious fight that we only imagined. To top off his look, was an old cowboy hat that made him look like a character out of TV.

"Cowboy's there!" We'd yell with excitement as we got close enough to see him.

"Don't bother him, *dejénlo*." Mommy would tell us. "He needs his privacy and doesn't want all of you kids hanging around him."

We loved talking to him because he would tell us all kinds of stories and make us all laugh.

"Why is he even here?" We'd ask Mommy.

"I don't know; he needs a place to stay for now."

We were always so curious and asked lots of questions.

"Doesn't he have a family? Where are they?"

Mommy quickly changed the subject. Driving into the brick layered driveway with grass growing in between the bricks, *Papi* parked the car right in front of my grandparent's house. The three wooden steps led to the side kitchen door that everyone used as the front door. It is where he was sitting. This was his favorite spot to sit so that he could watch everyone come and go. We all got out of the car one by one and had to sidestep around him to get inside.

"Hi Cowboy!" we'd say, but he wouldn't even flinch.

"*Saluden primero,*" Mommy would tell us.

We knew that we had to go inside and say hello to our grandparents first. One by one we'd go and give *Mama* Jesusa a hug and kiss and then *Papa* Maximiliano as well. First Johnny, then Diana, me, Keki, and finally Eli, and everyone else took turns in saying hello properly. Walking into the tiny frame house, I always wondered how we could get all of our family in there when we would all get together. We had over fifty-one cousins.

"*Hasta que vinieron a vernos; ya se estaban tardando. Estaba contando los días.*"

Mama Jesusa always counted the days that we didn't visit them and would let us know how many days had gone by when we did go. It wasn't that she didn't have visitors since there was always someone at her house. They were always excited to see Keki and Eli; they were the little ones. They usually had to stay inside with Mommy, and then I, Diana, and Johnny would run outside. Huddling around Cowboy, we'd sit on the steps with him.

"Stop staring at him!" Johnny would always get mad at me about something.

"I'm not staring; I'm just looking at him. Ask him to open a soda bottle, please." I ran inside and found a bottle in the kitchen. "Cowboy, please open."

I handed him the bottle as my brother and sister gave me a look. He grabbed the bottle and raised it up to his mouth while we bit hard on our lips. He placed the cap in his mouth between his top and bottom front teeth and "Pop!" The bottle cap flew off. That was always worth it.

The new car was packed up and off we were to the big city leaving our home and extended family behind. For Mommy, leaving the family was very difficult especially since her parents, *Mama* Jesusa and *Papa* Maximiliano, were elderly, much older than my other grandparents. My mom was one of the youngest in her family of ten siblings being number eight to be exact in the lineup. This side of the family has always had many festive gatherings with lots of food, music, and many, many cousins. At one time we were over fifty first cousins not to mention second who were as close as our first. We all used to love to gather at *Mama* Jesusa's house with all of the cousins, *tías*, *tíos*, and other extended family.

At one of our gatherings, the cousins were out in the street of Los Torritos under the light while June bugs kept buzzing all around us right in front of the Rubio's church. We used to hang out in the street while our moms and dads were visiting inside *Mama* Jesusa's house.

"How can they possibly go to church for that long?"

"No, Mommy says that *son de la religión*."

"We know that, but how can they only wear dresses and not jeans?"

"No, they can't wear make-up, or even dye their hair."

"I can't go without wearing my jeans; they're like the most comfortable, they're like pajamas."

"When I grow up I have to dye my hair; I'm not going to want gray hair." Bibi said, as she undid her ponytail from its thick rubber band.

One of my best friends attended the church across the street from my grandmother's house.

I told my cousins, "Hey—don't let the religion fool you." "She's fun to be with, and if it weren't for the dress you wouldn't even know."

"Yeah, but they go to church for about four hours, and I hate to wear dresses."

"How can they stand that?"

"Don't you know they take breaks?"

"You don't know anything."

Their religion made us so curious about everything that we would sit outside and talk for hours. It was during these conversations that we decided to count just how many cousins we had in our family. Usually it would be Bibi, Lali, and me because all of us were the same age.

Well…I'd start "There's TaTa …"

"No, no, she hates for anyone to call her that, remember she wants us to call her Adelita, not TaTa."

Bibi chimed in protecting her older sister.

"No-one has ever called her that; what are you even talking about? She's TaTa, and she'll always be TaTa. *Bueno,* then there's Fita, and don't tell me she doesn't want to be called that either because I'll stop right here."

"No, just stop it! She doesn't care."

Bibi was the youngest of seven children in her family and defended all of them. It would never fail; she would turn into a pit-bull sometimes.

Then Lali adds, "What about your name, Bibi or Bibitita."

As we would start giggling Bibi would get mad at us because we knew that only the family called her Bibitita, but everyone called her Bibi. Actually, it was supposed to be Benita, but we pronounced it Bibi so that was what we called her. Her brothers and sisters always babied her and called her "Bibitita," and we loved to make fun of her for that. The three of us always had a special connection because we would imagine our moms being pregnant together and then we would all start to giggle at the thought.

"*Ay, ¿estas, hora que tienen?*" our moms would tell us.

All of us were born in August just days apart in Mercedes, except for Lali who was born in Florida because her dad was stationed there at that time. She would always tell us that she wished she had been named Loulani instead of Delores.

"You wish!" We'd tell her, "Have you ever heard of a Mexican American named Loulani?"

We had names for most of our cousins. There was Yaya, Fita, Lena and Monny. There was also Mati, Mili, Meli, Nacho, *La* Flaca, Tuti and Mani. Also, my *tías* and *tíos* were Flaco, Cheta, *El* Red, Meme, Licha and Tavo. Also, Toti, Chepo, Chencha and Chacha. These are the ones that I can think of—and I promise that I'm not making any of them up. But Loulani, no I've never heard of a Mexican American named like that.

Music would be overflowing throughout the neighborhood at every gathering. *Papa* Maximiliano was a popular musician known for his talent throughout the Valley. *Músicos* would come from as far as Starr County to play with him and to hear him play his violin and mandolin. As he would play with his *músicos*, *Mama* Jesusa would be busy making *menudo* and *tamales* in the kitchen with my *tías*. We would run in and out slamming the front door.

We'd hear, "*¡No corran, callen!*" as we'd continue running through the house and exit through the back door. We used to love to go into the back room that was usually dark and filled with soaps that *Mama* Jesusa would make herself.

One of the *tías* would usually catch us and yell, "*No deben de estar jugando aquí, ándale vámonos,*" so we'd run out.

Then we'd run over to the chicken coop and the end of the winding trail that was at the back of the yard and count all of the eggs that had been laid. I never knew how all of us could fit in *Mama* Jesusa's tiny frame house for all of those celebrations. Still, my mommy would be leaving all of that for the unknown now and placing us in a city with entirely no relatives to visit. We'd be alone.

Every time my *Tía* Malena or as the other relatives would call her Lena, *Tío* Meme and their kids, my cousins, would come down from San Antonio, *Mama* Jesusa pulled out the red carpet—Valley style by making *menudo* for Memito, my oldest cousin. She would start the day before they would arrive by having Mommy or *Tía* Licha take her to Robles Supermarket, where all the workers knew my grandmother by name, to get the necessary ingredients for her famous *menudo*.

"*¿Cómo está, Doña Jesusa, viene Lena?*" The checkout clerk would ask her.

"Viene mañana; hay que comenzar hoy, preparando."

She was like a beautiful flower reaching up to the sun and dancing with excitement. My grandmother definitely wanted to dance.

The day of their arrival she'd start bright and early in the morning by cleaning the *menudo*, cutting it up into bite size perfect square pieces, and preparing the pigs feet so they could start boiling slowly to get them nice and soft.

As *Mama* Jesusa would say, *"No es menudo si no usan las patas de marrano."*

According to her that was the best part of the dish, so it was always a daylong process for it to cook properly. Then, while that would simmer, she would go down the list so that everyone would be called making sure all of the family would show up for the welcoming celebration. *Tío* Flaco, *Tía* Cheta, *Tío* Milo, *Tía* Julia, *Tío* Red, *Tía* Mary, *Tía* Licha, Mommy, *Tía* Lena, *Tío* Beto, of course she couldn't forget *Tío* Cheo, *Tía* Chacha, and *Tía* Chencha because they were the same as the *tías* and *tíos*.

"Ya viene Lena en camino—Y estoy haciendo menudo para Memito. Vengan todos."

Everyone would show up at the corner of Los Torritos and wait and wait for the San Antonio clan to arrive. The smell of the spicy cayenne pepper and mixed spices in the *menudo* permeated through the tiny white frame house crowded with family, and flowed out through the front screen door down the three wooden steps and all through the front yard and street where most of the many, many cousins were playing. The tempting smell would tease us as it tickled our noses and tantalized us.

Meanwhile, the *tías* stood in the tiny kitchen making corn *tortillas* and cutting up lime slices while laughing and sharing stories about all of us while preparing for the feast.

"*¿Supieron que hizo la Fita?*" My *Tía* Julia would start her story about my cousin.

"*Platícanos*" the *tías* would encourage her to tell them what she did as they shared stories about each of us.

No one would dare eat until Memito arrived.

"Why do we have to wait? You know I love *menudo* Mommy."

Mommy would look at me and explain, "He lives very far away, and when he comes, *Mama* Jesusa likes to make this special food for him to welcome them. She knows he likes it."

"But I love it more than he does. Why doesn't she ever make it for me?" Mommy laughed and *Mama* Jesusa said that she would make it for me later.

Just then we heard someone yelling, "¡*Ya vienen!* ¡*Ya vienen!*"

Finally, they had arrived. The entire Rentería family ran out to the street to welcome the long awaited *primos*. We could see them as they made their way onto the dirt drive up entrance, the heads and hands waving at us sticking out of the back windows.

"Is the *menudo* ready? I can smell it!" Memito yelled out.

He had no idea how much effort *Mama* Jesusa had put into it to make it just right and have it taste so amazing. One by one they stepped out of their green station wagon, *Tía* Lena, *Tío* Meme, Memito, Oscarito, Alberto, Carmela, and Victoria. My out of town cousins were here; my torture was over, and now we would get to eat our *menudo*. The celebration at Los Torritos could finally begin.

Lightning

Across the street from us lived my *Papi's* cousin Chema, Beto and their five kids, Lino, Betito, DeeDee, Lilly, and Letty. Chema and *Papi* were very close because they grew up together and were the same age. *Amá* Magda and Chema's dad *Tío* Tiko, were brother and sister. *Tío* Tiko would always come and visit us and tell us stories about when *Papi* was growing up.

"Toni era el mejor troquero manejando los troques cuando estaba chico, y tenía nomas doce años," my *tío* would tell us.

He would go on telling us how our dad would drive across the country in the big trucks hauling loads of cotton, onion, or whatever was being picked at the time. The families would travel up north together that's why they were all very close. My *Tía* Chema and *Papi* were like brother and sister so all of her kids were our cousins. We were lucky because they lived right across the street from us, and we got to play with them whenever we wanted. Lino was Johnny's age and Betito was my age, and they both liked to play baseball with Johnny. Sometimes, they would let the rest of us play with them when they couldn't get the other boys in the neighborhood to play with them. We would go across the street in the field where the golfers would practice their golf game and lay out our bases. This time when we were going to play baseball we all noticed that there were horses in the field.

"Whose horse is that?"

"What's it doing here?"

"Is it friendly?"

"Can I ride it?" We were all full of questions when Betito answered us.

"That's Lightning! He's my horse, and I don't think you want to ride him…not yet anyway. I'll let you know when he's ready."

Betito would ride horses at our uncle's home and had a special way of handling them. He had a gift with animals.

"This one is pretty cranky; *tío* wants me to break him in and then let him know when he's ready. He's supposed to pay me extra to get him real tame that's why he brought him over here. I'll be working extra hard with him."

All of us went over to look at Lightning where Betito had him fenced like he was an exhibit at a zoo, but he jolted and started jumping and neighing at us.

"Do you think he's scared of you?" I asked Betito.

"Well, he doesn't know me yet, but he'll get to know me pretty well soon enough."

"Are you scared of him?"

"Me, no way!"

I leaned into the fence reaching towards Lightning, and he quickly sprang up on his hind legs waving his front legs up and down in the air like weapons. I backed up and then ran screaming.

He apparently didn't like us. We just started laughing, thinking it was funny and then ran towards the makeshift baseball field.

"Let's play!" Johnny yelled. "Enough with the horse."

The next afternoon, Elena, my uncles' fiancé and our

church choir director picked us up for choir practice. I yelled over to Betito.

"Are you coming with us to practice?"

"Not today, I have to work with Lightning; he's doing great today!"

Elena took Keki and me to practice across town. We loved Elena, she was beautiful, tall, smart, and could sing and play the piano like a famous star. Most importantly, she was so nice to us and didn't even mind spending time with a bunch of kids.

"Okay, kiddos, let's take it from the top. Remember we're going to sing the entire song in *español*."

All of the songs that we sang were in Spanish, but we didn't mind. We wore beautiful long white robes like angels and had a reserved place where we stood in the front of the church during mass. We were all special because we were in the children's choir. Elena made us all feel like we had auditioned and gotten the special parts.

That day when we were returning from practice, I had an eerie feeling in the pit of my stomach as if something was about to happen but figured it was just a stomach ache. As we arrived close to our house, we could see that something terrible had happened but we couldn't tell exactly what. All of the neighbors had gathered outside of my home and were circled around our two cars that were parked by the curb on the side of the street where *Papi* and Mommy always parked them. The Zuniga's were there. So were the Barrera's and the Cuellar's. I could see the De La Guerra's in the street along with the Garza's and the Reyes'. In the middle of them was a police car and an ambulance parked in the street with their lights on and sirens blaring full blast.

"What happened? What's going on?" I cried asking Elena.

"Hold on *m'ijita*; let me park."

We ran out of the car then stopped as if we had seen a ghost, when we finally saw what all of the people were blocking from our sight.

"Oh my God! Betito!"

My ten-year-old cousin laid mangled in a pool of blood atop the roof of *Papi*'s car unconscious, as the paramedics were trying to revive him, and police were getting my shocked neighbors away from the scene. *Papi*'s car was completely smashed in like a pancake, windows all broken, glass scattered everywhere, and bloodstained throughout. That was only *Papi*'s car. Mommy's old blue Batmobile was in even worse shape. Mommy came running towards us and took us inside the house.

"Don't let them see any of this Elena! Take them inside!"

Elena grabbed Keki's hands and mine and did what Mommy said crying as she ran up the steps on the porch.

"Hurry girls!"

"No! I don't want to go inside! I want to see Betito! I want to go with *Papi*."

I insisted on staying outside to see what was going to happen with my cousin. Why should I be shielded from what was going on?

"Inside! Now!"

Elena insisted and took us inside. I started crying inside, and Elena tried to make me feel better by telling me that Betito would go to the hospital, and the doctor would take the best care of him there. We heard the sirens fade away, and *Papi* and Mommy came inside.

"He's going to be fine," *Papi* said.

"*Pobrecita* Chema." Lightning went crazy when Betito was working with him, and he couldn't control him.

"He went wild…jumping on your Mommy's car then he jumped on my car, and Betito fell off on top of it. Just jumping from one car to another that horse—then Lightening ran off to the field after that. Lino was finally able to stop him, but he had to shoot him because he was in such bad shape. Thank God that Betito landed on my car and not on the street or who knows what could have happened to him. He's going to have to have surgery though—lost lots of blood, and be in the hospital for a while, but he'll be okay. We're going to need new cars, but we'll figure that out." Elena took us to the hospital to visit Betito a few days later, and we took him a present and cards from the choir. He stayed in the hospital for many weeks.

As beautiful as horses are, they almost took my cousin's life. I never saw horses the same after the experience with Lightning.

L*as Mañanitas*

Sure enough, the dogs started barking on cue. The sun was just beginning to crack through the horizon as Bert began to shake me.

"They're here wake up!" Quickly, I jumped up to grab my camera telling him, "Call the boys." Running over to the door in my pajamas half asleep, I open the door. There they stood in the cool, rainy *madrugada* with guitars strumming.

"*Qué linda está la mañana, en que vengo a saludarte...*" my two brothers and my cousins sang to me. They had driven from San Antonio where they now live, to come serenade their loved ones here in the Valley for Mother's Day. Since I live in Edinburg, I was the last stop for them on their way back home. As they said their goodbyes, I gestured to my sons how it was now up to them to continue that tradition that had been passed down in our family for generations.

"We will, Mom; we will, don't worry."

Growing up, we never knew that Mommy was such a special mom. Most kids never realize how special their moms are until they become adults. It was always the night before Mother's Day that was a sleepless night for the entire family. Our bedroom was right next to the street with our two windows open because we didn't have air conditioning. If we were lucky, we got to put a fan in the window for cool air during the hot nights. The hum that it made would put me to sleep along with the random bark and howl of the neighborhood dogs.

Without fail on that particular May night just as we were all falling into dreamland the choirs of harmonious dogs would start their barking startling us back into reality.

"Why are all the dogs barking? What's going on?" We started to wake up after we were just beginning to fall asleep and the three of us seemed very confused.

"I was asleep! Why are y'all waking me up?"

It was already very late in the night when outside our window we heard a guitar playing and then someone singing. Jumping to my knees and peeking out of our window I could see figures in the darkness.

"It's our Uncle Saul and his *compadres*!" Diana jumped up on the bed.

"Listen they're here for Mommy!"

I grabbed my pillow and covered my head with it. Not wanting to listen to Spanish songs all night, I tried to go back to sleep; it was impossible, the singing was so loud, and the guitars and accordions sounded so awesome. Oh well, I joined my sisters and stuck my elbows on the windowsill looking out at the musicians just listening in awe. All the lights in the house were turned on by now. Mommy and *Papi* were standing by their window taking it all in arm in arm, and Johnny and Eli had come into our room and jumped on our bed. The show had begun. We knew it was going to be an all-nighter.

Sure enough, as we were listening to Uncle Saul, across the street at the Zuñiga's house you could hear Mrs. Zuñiga's very own *mariachi's* singing to her outside her window. They were now competing with our uncle and his musicians.

"Wow! They have trumpets!"

Johnny made the comment and noted how he could also hear several other *serenatas* throughout the neighborhood.

"Listen, it's like a band competition in the middle of the night."

Papi went outside to thank his brother and the other *músicos* and invite them in. You could hear them through the window.

"*Pásenle,*" *Papi* told his little brother.

"*No, Toni, tenemos muchas casas y madres que visitar.*"

Off they went with guitars and accordions in hand. Their next stop was directly across the street to our *Tía* Chema's. As we continued to listen, then another group pulled up to our house. This time it was Mommy's Cousin Eloy and his band. At the same time that Chema was being serenaded, Mrs. Zuñiga and everyone else in the neighborhood were being serenaded, and Cousin Eloy and band serenaded Mommy. We watched and listened through our windows and even danced about in our bedroom. Then we watched as *Papi* talked to them outside for a minute, and they too turned down his invitation to come in because they had too many other homes to visit. *Papi* came back inside to talk to us.

"This is a special night. There will probably be other musicians coming by and it is imperative that they are properly thanked and acknowledged. They stay up all night to serenade the mothers who are important to them on this special night. That is a very special gift."

The *serenatas* went on all night long. After Cousin Eloy and his band, then *Tío* Red and his group came, after that group came then the other *tíos* would come. Altogether, Mommy would average about five or six *serenatas* every Mother's Day eve. Even the dogs stopped barking.

The Attic

When we first arrived in Houston, *Papi* ended up renting a house right next to Hobby Airport, which was off of Telephone Road, until he and Mommy could find something permanent for us. I thought it was the best house ever with a large front yard and all sorts of jungle-like bushes shaped like mysterious caves in the backyard and perfect for us to play hide and seek in. There was a long gravel driveway lined with forest like trees at the entrance that seemed like miles until we reached our temporary home. The best part of the house was the eerie garage that we weren't supposed to venture into. That of course was way too tempting. As you walked in, there was a hanging chunky old rope that could be pulled on with a big, wooden foldable ladder that would come down from the opening in the ceiling. This was off limits. However, being the curious kids that we were, we couldn't resist not knowing what was up there. We had to know. The rope was extremely large, bulky and heavy, especially for a seven-year-old to pull down alone.

"Johnny, please help me pull the rope so we can see what's up there. Don't you want to know?"

He was curious too, but far more responsible and didn't want to get in trouble.

"We're not supposed to go up there. We should wait until *Papi* gets home so that he can go with us." He and Diana were always so bossy.

"I just want to see." He looked at me and grabbed the rope.

"Well, then you owe me big time." He yanked on the rope, and the ladder came down. We looked up into the opening and it was dark.

"Go ahead." My big brother gestures me with his hand for me to go first.

As we climbed up the ladder, the light began to fade. The attic was extremely dark, mysterious and very scary. All around were old boxes and crates full of stuff, all kinds of stuff. There were statues, dishes, and so many things that we didn't know what to look at first.

"I told you there'd be exciting stuff up here. I just knew it! We have to go and get Diana and Keki, so they can see all this stuff. They'll want to come play up here."

Our discovery then became our favorite secret play area. We couldn't let Mommy find out that we would go up into the attic because she would definitely get mad at us, so we would sneak up there whenever we would play outside. Johnny would help us pull the rope and unfold the enormous wooden ladder so that we could climb up into our secret playroom. We would pretend to be in another time and place. Then we'd get snapped out of our pretend world.

"I told you not to go up there! ¡*Caranchos, nunca entienden*!" Mommy would yell at us. Somehow, she had found out about our secret.

"Please help me pull the rope down," I would ask Johnny. "I want to go up there!"

"No. Mom said no." He would always get after me for everything.

We stayed at this house until the end of the summer. It was at this in between home that we ended up witnessing the first walk on the moon by Neil Armstrong on our black and white TV set while my mommy was in the hospital with her first bout of cancer. We all huddled around our tiny TV sitting on the floor cheering as Armstrong set foot on the moon saying his famous words, "That's one small step for man, one giant leap for mankind."

My *tías*, Fita and Cheta alternated taking care of us that summer. It was also that summer that I ended up continuing to go up into the forbidden attic because I discovered that I was strong enough to pull the big rope all by myself with determination. That one afternoon I felt extremely brave that I gave the rope a quick yank and jerk when suddenly SNAP! It broke right off of the ladder and the huge wooden ladder came crashing down smack dab on my nose knocking me out on the floor. Blood splattered everywhere, screams and cries filled across the front yard, through the house, and into Mommy's ears. I was finally able to get everyone's attention. Mommy grabbed me off of the floor and ran with me to the neighbors' house. She just happened to be some nurse, or medical assistant, and told Mommy that I would eventually be fine, so I wasn't taken to the doctor. My nose was broken, and she said it would heal. I never played in the attic after that. My nose was swollen purple for weeks.

No Spanish

We were five. Johnny my oldest brother, Diana my oldest sister, then me the middle child, followed by Keki, my youngest sister, and Eli my youngest brother who was only three years old when we moved to Houston. We grew up speaking Spanish then English, even though *Papi* had a college degree. When I started school I remember being shocked at not being allowed to speak Spanish. If we'd dare to utter a word in our own language, we would surely be punished by being sent to the principal's office.

"It will not be tolerated," Mrs. Sanders would tell the class.

Many of the kids in my class would get sent to the office because they would say something to each other in Spanish.

"*¿Qué dijo?*" Juan whispered across to Tony's desk.

"I've told you kids, no Spanish—I'll have to send you to the office."

Slowly she put the piece of white chalk down in mid-sentence, and she walked over to her desk to get the pad of referral slips to the principals' office. They were always easily accessible and within reach so that all of us knew that we could be next to go. So off she would send Juan to the principals' office, and a few minutes later he would come back with tears in his eyes trying not to cry and holding his back pockets. The rest of us in class would be terrified wondering what had happened to Juan.

"For sure he got a few licks," Tony said. That's what always happens.

At that time all the teachers were just like Mrs. Sanders—white. At the time of the move, my youngest brother was only three years old, and he only spoke Spanish.

The strange part of this is that now I am the mother of four sons. Two are in college and two still live at home. My oldest son is now proficient in Spanish among other languages but not because he learned it at home. He has always asked me why he and his brothers were not taught Spanish along with English. "It would have been so much easier for us if we had spoken it at home like you did, Mom."

I just couldn't do that to them. The memory of being punished for speaking the forbidden language at school embedded deeply in my mind that I didn't want my children to have those barriers. At the same time though, I didn't realize that I was hindering them. I wish now that I would have engaged them in my native tongue more so. Regardless, they are managing and learning it alongside their peers at school.

Right before school started in the late sixties, my parents moved us into the most beautiful three bedroom, two-bath, red brick house in a very nice neighborhood with perfect sidewalks lining the suburbia street. Our home had a two-car garage, long paved driveway, a fenced backyard, and was half a block away from our school. I had never seen such a perfect neighborhood before, except on shows like *The Brady Bunch*.

"We must be rich," I said to my dad.

"Of course we're not. Why do you say that?"

"Well, our house has TWO bathrooms!"

That was a huge deal for us. Actually, he had gotten a new job at the University of Houston. It was going to be a step up for *Papi* to begin and start up the HEP program (High School Equivalency Program). He would work with migrants and drop out students to help them get their degrees. At the same time he was also working on his doctorate. While he began his new job, all of us got to go to a brand-new school and found out that we were the only ones like us. This was not at all like the Valley. People looked and talked differently than we did. It was a total shock. Not only in school, but also in our neighborhood we seemed to be the only Mexican Americans. It was unusual for us because where we lived before, everyone was just like us. For the first time in my life I was experiencing the feeling of being a minority. At this time, I was too young to realize the significance of what we were about to witness living in Houston. It was one of the largest cities in the nation as well as one of the most racially segregated school districts at the time. Unbeknownst to us kids, we were flung into one of history's most controversial public schools' decisions—busing.

This was a time when students were discovering their identities and standing up for their heritage. Students were protesting and holding sit-ins resulting from segregation issues still looming from *Brown v. The Board of Education* (1959). Yet, the public schools were not integrated. Most schools were either all white or all black. Houston attempted to remedy this by first only placing black administrators and teachers in white schools and vice versa, but there were protests. Then busing students miles across town to mix up the schools' demographics began, and parents as well as students began to protest and walk out. Meanwhile, we were in the middle of all of it.

Being a seven-year-old, I did not understand what was going on. I just quietly went to my new school with my sisters and was very excited to meet my new friends. They were not at all like my friends back home, but I got used to them and most of them were helpful to me.

There were many firsts for us at our Houston home. Skating was a first. Not only would I skate up and down the perfect sidewalks that lined the homes of our street, but I also learned to skate backward as well. All of the kids in the neighborhood would skate. We never did that in the Valley because we didn't have sidewalks to skate on. The neighbors also had talent shows for all of the kids. They would organize them and have us all sign up with what we were going to do.

As several kids lined up in front of Robins' house, I nervously practiced my song over and over in my head. Robin was my friend from school and also lived on the corner at the end of the street. She was an only child and had everything anyone could imagine. I loved going to her house to play; there were always so many choices for us. Her name was a bit funny, but it matched her because she would always wear high ponytails and fancy dresses with colorful knee-high socks that always matched. Robin was a bit on the heavy side and didn't like running games much, but she was very popular. Since she was the popular one in the neighborhood, she would have the talent show at her house.

I was getting nervous about my act. It was the song that we had learned in class and was my favorite especially since I knew all of the words. It was so exciting—we never did things like this in the Valley. Sure, we would play outside. That was fun, but never talent shows. As Robins' mom called my name, I went up to the front of her driveway.

I introduced myself…stated what I was going to do and proceeded to sing "He's got the whole world in his hands," until I finished. I was very proud of myself.

Next, my little sister Keki went up and sang, "A tisket a tasket, a yellow flowered basket."

Mommy had fixed up a basket with flowers from the yard to be thrown out as she walked around the driveway and sang. She looked ridiculously cute with her bouncy golden curls and her yellow dress to match the basket. Everyone loved her. After all of the kids were done everyone got little ribbons. Keki won the talent show though, and I have to admit I was jealous.

Halloween was also a big deal with all the homes getting involved decorating and some even creating haunted houses. It was a fun neighborhood. It was very different from our Valley neighborhood. That was fun also. We would play *"el bote"* until late in the night or until Mommy called us inside. You could hear someone kicking the can and everyone screaming and laughing outside. I used to hate being sick because listening to the laughing and shouting of the kids through the window would be torture for me. We didn't play the same games, and the kids looked different, but it was still fun at our Houston home. We were learning new things. One we already knew was not to speak Spanish.

School In Houston

I often share with my sons the feeling of what it was like attending that school in Houston. It was a mainly white school. My teacher was black because that year the city was beginning to bus students into some of the schools to try and mix up the demographics. We as children were unaware of the repercussions, but there were many protests as a result of these actions, and many people were extremely upset with the schools and the situation. I had never been around people of so many different colors or cultures before because we were isolated to only our small town. Mrs. Knoll was my third-grade teacher, and she was very nice. In the Valley, most everyone was either Mexican American or White, but mainly Mexican American. Growing up in Weslaco, we never had the opportunity of meeting kids of other cultures in the sixties and seventies. It wasn't that we didn't want to, it was just that our Valley was very much separated from the rest of the nation at that time.

When we did leave for Houston we all began to see everything differently. The world began to open up when I was in the third grade. I was nervous about going to my new school even though it was right across the street from our new house. All the kids would be new, and my friends were all at Weslaco. We all walked across the street to the new school together in the morning, Diana, me, and Keki because Eli was only three years old and not old enough to go to school yet. We went to our different classrooms. Diana was in the fifth-grade hall, I was in the third-grade hall, and Keki was in the Kindergarten hall. First, we had to walk Keki to her class because she was a baby, and she would cry if we made her walk all by herself to her classroom. Then Diana and I went to our classrooms. My classroom was right across from the girls' bathrooms, which made it easy to find, and it was at the very end of the hall.

All the kids in my class were nice and made friends with me rather fast. Their names were Todd, Valerie, Elaine, and Leonard, different than my friends in the Valley. They were also all white. There was one other Mexican American girl in my class. I couldn't understand why she hated me.

"Who do you think you are?" Tina would ask me in a *chola*, gangster voice with a look that meant she wanted to beat me up.

"I'm not doing anything to you; please just leave me alone. We can be friends if you'd like."

Trying my best I would find a way to talk to her, but nothing would work. She just hated me.

"You think you're better than me don't you because those white kids are friends with you. They're just using you.

They don't like you."

Then she would push me and start calling me names.

"You're just a ... That's all you are, and you'll never be anything else! Don't you forget it!"

"Stop it! Stop it, Tina!"

I ran away from her, but she ran after me yelling at me.

"Just because your skin is white like theirs! You're still a Mexican!"

"I know I am!" I would yell back at her as I ran away. "I know I'm a Mexican."

I ran crying to find Mrs. Knoll our black teacher to tell her how Tina kept being mean to me. Spotting her across the playground, I dashed to her as my bully was watching me the entire time. Not caring I continued on my mission and pushed my tears aside telling my teacher about how I had been bullied. "Now, now child, calm down. We shall take care of this. Don't you worry."

Mrs. Knoll was the sweetest teacher ever. She took Tina aside, and that afternoon *Papi* was in the principal's office talking about what had happened. Tina never bothered me again, but she wouldn't talk to me, and she would look at me funny. The white kids were all nice and got along well with me; they were all my friends.

To this day, I never forget the hateful, hurtful things that she would say about me for no reason at all. My *Papi* had to go to the principals' office many times while we lived in Houston. Not that we were bad or misbehaved. We were always good kids. It was just that many things were done so differently at our new school, and *Papi* didn't think we were being treated fairly.

Coming home from school Friday afternoon, I was excited about the project that our teacher Mrs. Knoll had assigned for the next several weeks.

"Children, I want for you to keep a diary and log everything that your family eats for dinner. We want to see how our families are at home with their children and if the parents are feeding them nutritious foods. You will turn in your diaries at the end of the third week." Mrs. Knoll told us that this would be an exciting assignment and that we would all learn about each other by writing everything down that all of us do at home.

"Mommy, I have a project that my teacher assigned us that will take me three weeks to do."

Of course, Mommy was in the kitchen getting started on dinner when we all got home after school.

"What kind of project?" She asked as she scooped the *manteca* out of the tub and started to knead it into the flour that was in the huge plastic green bowl. The next day *Papi* went to talk to Mrs. Knoll, and she changed our project.

Johnny started attending the junior high close by our home. It was a very big school; I know because I remember going to visit it before school started. My parents became worried of the violence at the school. Apparently, students were starting to take weapons to school. Busing was in full swing at this junior high, and all of the students were upset as well as their parents. It had been an all-white school the year before, but now black students were being brought in from other districts so that students could be blended. The black students didn't like being integrated with the white students and vice versa. Mommy and *Papi* didn't want my brother in an environment with so much controversy. So, they did what was very hard to do—they sent him back home where he would be safe, to live with *Amá* Magda in the Valley. My brother spent the second year of junior high in the Valley, and he became part of the *Familia* Santos at least part-time. That meant that every other weekend we would go home to see him and the family. The seven-hour trip got to be shorter and shorter as we made it more and more often. This was perfect for Mommy because she was able to see her son, her parents, and her extremely huge family. But, as the year went on, Mommy's father *Papá* Maximiliano started to get sick.

By the time fourth grade began, we had adjusted to our new Houston lifestyle. It was very different from the Valley. Our school was still behind with busing, and it was predominantly white except for the principal and teachers. My classroom had about thirty students that were all white except for Tina who did not like me at all. That was fine with me because I blended in well with all of the white kids and she didn't.

Some weekends we would go down to the Valley to see the *familia,* and my cousins would give us all a hard time because they thought we were different.

"I'm the same! Can't you see?" I'd tell them as we gathered at *Mama* Jesusa's house.

"You sound different and you act different. That big city is changing you—all of you."

I felt sad that they thought that. Why were they acting different with us? I was still the same person.

"You're acting all *gring*a now. *Se te olvidó el español.*"

My *primos* were a bit tough at first, but so was everyone else. When you're a Mexican American it's understood that you speak Spanish. You're judged by your peers and looked at in a certain way if you do not fit in. We were trying to fit into both worlds that didn't seem too accepting.

Amá Magda's house was much different though because my favorite aunt lived there. My *Tía* Cheta was everyone's favorite because she did everything with us like play games with us and pop fireworks in the street during New Year's Eve and take us anywhere that we wanted to go. She was the cool aunt. She was all of the cousins' favorite aunt. She was my favorite aunt. Sometimes *Tía* Cheta would call me *La Flaca* because I was always so skinny or *La Wedincha* because my skin was so light.

My *tía* could have had her mechanic shop because she taught me everything about the car.

"*Mira m'ijita,* this is where you check the oil. You pull this out and wipe it clean with a rag. Then you put it back in and pull it out again. It will show you right here how much oil you have." As she pointed to the line on the stick she said, "You see. *Tienes que saber.*"

She then continued to show me the spark plugs and where you connect the battery. Every time that we'd go to *Amá* Magda's she'd teach me something.

"It doesn't matter that you're a girl. *La mujer no puede depender nomás en el hombre. Aprende hacer todo sola.*" She was very smart, and I always listened to her.

Politics was something that she enjoyed and knew much about, and she would teach us everything that she could. On one of the walls in her house you could go through the history of all the past presidential elections, governor, and local elections posted along with articles of headlines of the day. The buttons of Kennedy for president, Johnson for president right next to Kennedy Is Shot in a newspaper clipping were neatly attached to the wall in the hall. Every time that I would go to *Amá* Magda's house that wall would draw my attention. My *Tía* Cheta would go over and explain the different paraphernalia to me with a story so that I could understand it. She always made politics exciting.

Other than politics, *Tía* Cheta would let us work in the *tiendita* behind the big counter.

"*Si te dicen nomás, apúntalo*—you write it down in this book."

My *tía* would get a big book from under the counter and open it up with different names from the neighborhood.

They didn't have to pay. We would just write down what they would take and their name with the total. They would pay when they could. That was their system, and it worked for them. Everyone from the *barrio* was like a big family. They just trusted all of them and believed that they would pay them when they could.

When we got back to Houston, it was back to school as usual. Now that I was in fourth grade my assignments were getting a bit harder, but I could handle it. What was getting a little hard to handle was the situation in the classroom with my classmates. I still had the same teacher from the previous year, Mrs. Knoll, and she was still super nice to everyone. I also had all of the same kids as the year before. For the most part they were all nice, except for Tina. She didn't like me, and she was the only other Mexican American in my class. Even though *Papi* had gone to the principal to talk to him and my teacher my third-grade year, she continued with her bullying behind everyone's back. I could either be friends with her or be friends with my white friends who were nice to me, so I chose to be friends with my white friends.

One day, Mrs. Knoll announced that we had a special paper to write.

"Class, I want for you to think of someone that is special to you besides your parents. Think of how this person has helped you or made a difference for you and write a paper about that person."

I knew exactly whom I wanted to write about. There was no question in my mind that I was going to write about my *Tía* Cheta.

"The other part class, is that you will have to read your paper up in front of the class."

Oh, no! I couldn't do that. I knew I could write about my *tía*, but I didn't want to have to get in front of the class and read it to all of my friends. What was I going to do? My white friends from Houston didn't understand things from the Valley. They didn't know what a *tía* was. They probably had never heard of a name Cheta before. What was I going to do? As it was that darn Tina already hated me and was making my life miserable. All I needed was one little tiny thing for her to grab onto and it would get out of control. I already knew her.

That day after school I walked home with my sisters since our home was directly across the street from the elementary school that we attended. When we got back, I excitedly told Mommy about the paper that I had to write for class.

"Wow! *¡Qué Bueno!*" She was very busy getting dinner ready for *Papi* and chasing after my little brother.

Diana, Keki, and I got out of the way and started our homework in our room. I quickly began to write my paper about my favorite person knowing that I had to read it aloud to the class and careful that my sisters could not see whom I was writing about.

We shared a room at this house also just like at our Weslaco house, but this room was much larger, and this house had two and one-half bathrooms which was an enormous difference. My parents had a bedroom with their very own bathroom. Then there was a bathroom in the hall for all of us to use. There was also a half bathroom next to the kitchen without a shower. We thought we were rich with so many bathrooms. This house was like a mansion.

The next day at school I was so nervous about reading my paper on my favorite person that my stomach was hurting, and I felt like I was going to be sick. Maybe if I tell Mrs. Knoll that I feel sick, she'll let me go to the nurse, and I won't have to read my paper. Then she started.

"Class, we're going to begin reading about your favorite person. Who wants to go first?"

I tried to hide so that she wouldn't call on me. Praying that she would forget that I was even in the class, I prayed to the Virgin so that I would not have to read my paper. Before I knew it, I felt sweat dripping down my arms, and my heart was beating so hard like a bass drum in a parade.

"Leonard, please read your paper to the class."

Thank God! Leonard read about his Boy Scout leader, and everyone applauded him as he smiled. I couldn't help but think that he looked so cute with his dimples when he smiled. Then Elaine went next with her pretty, long, light brown hair nicely pulled back and her mini dress and white knee-high socks. She was one of my best friends. Then one of the two Debbies read her paper. One of them was very funny with short blonde hair and the other one was skinny and a bit annoying with longer blonde hair. Both of them were nice to me. Then Todd was next, the most popular boy in the class. All the girls seemed to like him for some reason. He had blonde hair and wore wire-rimmed glasses. Although he was nice, I really didn't see what the big deal was about him. After half the class had gone, it was my turn. I took a deep breath, did the sign of the cross, and walked up to the front of the class with my paper in my hand. I looked at Mrs. Knolls and then at my white classmates except for Tina and then looked at my paper and began.

My favorite person is my Aunt Charlotte...and proceeded to tell them about *Tía* Cheta. They would not understand the real version about my *tía*. I couldn't tell them about how her real name is Carlotta. Or that she calls me *La Flaca,* or *Wedincha,* or *M'ijita.* I couldn't tell them about how she tells me to just *apúntalo* in the book. I couldn't tell them how she would tell me *that la mujer tiene que saber como hacer todo.* They wouldn't understand. None of them are like me so how could they understand? Maybe Tina would, but I didn't care what she thought because she hated me. All of my classmates seemed to like my Aunt Charlotte though, except for Tina. I don't think she would have liked my *Tía* Cheta either.

Rockstar

One of the best parts of living in the Valley was that we lived so close to the beach. South Padre Island was only an hour away from our house and when summertime came around *Papi* would always take us to our favorite places there to spend the day. Mommy would pack up our lunches of bologna and potted meat sandwiches and the ice chest with Shasta drinks while we'd get our swimsuits on. That was all we needed. Crowded into our blue Batmobile, off we'd go. The hour-long trip seemed as if it took forever.

"Are we almost there?" We'd keep asking *Papi*.

"No, not yet. When you start to see water that means we're almost there."

We had to pass all of the Valley cities along Expressway 83 and then Highway 100 to get to the island. First was Mercedes, where Mommy liked to go for groceries at Foodland. On some Saturday mornings we all got to tag along to the trip to Mercedes for grocery shopping. The big store on Texas Blvd. had a large parking lot with mechanical rides at the entrance that we all wanted to ride on. Eli was usually the only one who got to ride on the little horsy. Inside the grocery store people quickly filled their shopping carts with all types of goodies including freshly baked *pan dulce*. We loved going to Foodland and would usually come back with a trunk full of yummy stuff.

The cities after Mercedes were not as well known to us, but they were La Feria, Harlingen, and San Benito. After that *Papi* would tell us that he'd be turning onto Highway 100, which led to the island. It was at this turn when he'd usually stop on the side of the road to buy a watermelon.

"Stop! *Papi*, stop!"

Slowly our car would pull over to the side of the road where a man would be selling watermelons in the back of his pick-up. *Papi* would let us get down with him to select the perfect watermelon, which he would do by tapping on it with his knuckles and listening to the sound.

"You hear that? This one sounds good. Look at the bottom of it. See how it's yellow; that means it's ready."

"*Nos gusta esta.*" He'd tell the man.

"*¿La quieres probar?*" The man would ask him.

"*Pues sí, vamos a ver.*"

Papi was always right about picking watermelon. The nice man picked up the fruit and cut a perfect triangle into it and presented it to *Papi* as if it were a present.

Taking a big bite he wiped his mouth with his white handkerchief with a cursive S on it that was always nicely pressed and looked at us saying, "Yup, that's really good."

As he paid our new friend we jumped back into the car telling Mommy that we had helped *Papi* pick out the perfect watermelon. Then we'd be off to our favorite destination, Andy Bowie.

"Look! I can see the water!"

We'd all start yelling as soon as we'd get to Laguna Vista because we knew we were getting close. Hanging out of the windows to feel the wind, Johnny, Diana, and I would lean our body out from the waist up and wave to the cars passing us by. "*¡Metánse ya!*"

Mommy would yell at us to get back in then it was back on the road, and before we knew it we were crossing the big, long bridge to get to the island. *Papi* drove straight to Andy Bowie and found the perfect place to park as we flew out of the car running towards the waves.

"Stop! ¡*Qué bárbaros!*"

Mommy would be yelling as we ran into the water. We would look as far as we could and still see blue water with white foamy waves forming on top that made it look like the ocean was alive and talking to us. What was it saying to us? The smell was strong and fresh that we just wanted to take it all in. As we turned around and looked back at the car with the trunk lifted up we could still see her yelling at us, but we couldn't hear her. Above her the seagulls were circling thinking that she might have food for them to scoop up. As they circled, she waved with her arms and other packed cars passed by trying to find the perfect place to set up their camp for the day. She always worried at the beach and wanted us to stay right at the edge of the water. That was no fun; we wanted to jump with the waves. We wanted to feel the white-water crash on our backs and knock us down with its full force. We wanted the ocean to come to life with us in it. Then we'd see her jumping up and down and waving her hands, so we had to go to her and listen to the lecture.

"*Ay, que niños,* do you want to go back home? *Vale más que no se vayan lejos.*"

Of course we didn't want to leave so we'd stay close by for a while and little by little the water would take us further and further away like a star in the sky that seems unreachable.

"We have to get back to where Mommy is." Diana would yell at us, "She's going to get so mad and want to take us home."

Grabbing my hand she'd pull me towards her so that we could make our way back to our headquarters, but it was much harder than we expected.

"Come on!"

"I'm trying!"

Our feet felt as if they had bricks tied to them because we couldn't lift them.

"We would come back looking like lobsters and fighting for the only shower in the house. The sunburn was bad enough, but the sand stuck to all of us felt like sandpaper. Then we'd have to wait hours for our turn to actually get in our one bathroom, but it was always worth it. It was so worth it.

The big city of Houston was so different from our small town in the Rio Grande Valley, but when *Papi* told us that he was taking us to the beach, it sounded like home to me.

"Get your swimsuits on; we'll be gone for the day!" *Papi* told us one Saturday morning.

"Yay!! We're going to South Padre Island!" We all started to yell.

"No, no, we're not going to the Valley. We're going to Galveston. It's right next to Houston. You all are going to love it. We have a surprise for you too."

"Surprise! What's the surprise?" We all started yelling and asking our dad what he and our mom were planning.

"You will all find out when we get there."

We had all woken up early to watch cartoons and were all stretched out on the living room floor eating our *taquitos* of potato and eggs with beans.

"Finish your *tacos* and put your plates away in the kitchen first," Mommy came in to tell us. With one hand on her hip and a kitchen spoon in the other she returned to the kitchen to finish cooking. She was preparing some lunches for later in the day and making breakfast for *Papi*.

"What do you think the surprise is?" I asked Diana and Johnny.

Putting my *taquito* down I said, "Probably they're going to tell us that we're moving back to the Valley." Never eating very much, I was always the picky eater as a child.

"Are you out of your mind?" My big brother said. "We just got here; we're not going back. Besides Dad has a good job here, and he's not giving it up just because you want to go back to the Valley. We have to get used to it here; get over it." My brother always said it like it was even though we didn't like it. "Then what is it? What are they going to tell us?"

By now Keki and Eli had already gone to get their swimsuits on and were ready to go. Being so young, they weren't that interested in our conversation about figuring out what might happen; they just wanted to get to the beach.

"Let's just go get ready." Diana started to give us orders with her authoritative voice.

"Wait…what if what they want to tell us is that they want to get a divorce? What are we going to do? I bet that's it! Mommy and *Papi* are going to get a divorce just like on TV and then we're going to have to choose between them."

All of a sudden, I was terrified because my mind kept going on and on making me think that it was possible.

"You don't even know what that means." Johnny said.

"Yes I do. I know what it means; some of my friends have parents that are divorced, and they don't like it."

He seemed surprised that I knew what I was talking about and opened his eyes wide to show that.

"Well our parents aren't like that. They're not at all like that. Let's just get our swimsuits on."

We ran to our rooms to get our suits on and decided not to worry about what the surprise was anymore.

When we got to the beach we noticed how different it was from our beach back home.

"Why is there a big wall? It looks weird." *Papi* explained to us that there had been a big hurricane that devastated the city and killed almost everyone living here so the citizens decided to build a wall to protect them from future storms.

"Our beach doesn't have a wall like that." Johnny pointed to the wall and noticed that there was also a street right in front of it also.

"No, ours doesn't have a wall, but it has dunes which protect as well and are natural."

Papi parked the car in a parking lot, and we ran through the sand to the water with Mommy running after us yelling for us not to go too far. There was no Andy Bowie, so we just played in the water for a while then went back to the car for lunch. Mommy had made some *taquitos* for us to eat.

After our *taco* lunch *Papi* drove to another place on the beach where there were lots of cars and people gathered. There was a stage and several tables on a large wooden deck right up close to the beach. From a distance we could see a band on the scene, but it was hard to see which band it was because there was a large crowd gathered around the stage.

"Wow! Are we going to get to go there and listen to the band?"

Johnny loved music probably more than anybody. He had all of the Beatle albums and had taught himself to play guitar.

"What band is it? It looks like they're Rock Stars!"

Papi looked over at Mommy, and they both smiled.

"This is your surprise."

As *Papi* parked the car all of us eagerly jumped out of the back seat. There were so many cars in the parking lot that Mommy was trying to keep us all together so that we wouldn't get lost. It was Galveston, not South Padre Island after all. While we're walking she explains to us how she wants us to behave because it's essential to her.

"We're going to see your cousin, and we haven't seen him in a while. He's doing so well, and I'm so proud of him."

We were so excited because Julio was one of our oldest cousins, and he was now a famous musician. He had made records, and they played on the radio. We knew that he would be famous.

"Look at all these people! He is a Rock Star!"

Finally we made it to the entrance of the large deck and managed to find a table towards the back of it. We could see Julio from where we were sitting, and he must have seen us as we walked in because he waved at us as he was singing one of his hit songs. With all of the girls Ooohing and Aaawing over him, and the guys wishing they could sing like he did, he continued with his next song.

"I'm going to dedicate this next song to my favorite aunt my *Tía* Eliza who came to see me all the way from the Rio Grande Valley! This one's for you *tía*!"

My cousin then sang my Mommy's favorite song by Engelbert Humperdinck. He was such a charmer and just knew stuff like that. Every time we'd be at *Mama* Jesusa's house and he'd show up he'd always tell my Mommy and my *tías* how pretty they looked, and he'd sing to them. My *tías* absolutely

106

loved him, and so did all of his cousins—like me. I always thought he was the most handsome person ever. Apparently, everyone else did too because everyone was going crazy yelling for him.

We were all so proud thinking, "Hey that's our *primo* up there." He sang, *"Please Release Me,"* which was the most popular song at that time. Mommy was so touched that we could see beads of tears rolling down her cheeks. "¡*Ay, que Julio!*" It was all she could say. As he finished the song he yelled out a hello to all of us as he waved to us.

"Those are all of my *primos* from the Valley!"

He then continued with his songs. When he took a short break, he came over to give Mommy a hug and kiss and say hello to all of us; then he had to run off, it was his calling—his purpose. We could hear the waves as the water hit the shore from where we were sitting; the sun was starting to go down.

What a beautiful end to a fascinating journey. ¡*Ay, que Julio!*

First Communion

Last year, my niece Maritza, became a full-fledged 100% member of the Catholic Church. When and if she ever finds someone who all of her relatives would approve of to be worthy of her, then she could marry in her church if however her hypothetical future fiancé were also a full-fledged 100% member of the Catholic Church. If not, then there'd be a problem.

She went against all of our beautifully artistic and religious culturally beliefs that we, her family, had all been raised with and shocked us all. There wasn't anything wrong with how she entered into the realm of the Holy Church, just a bit different. Completely out of her control, my sister and brother in law went through many hardships that interfered with my niece following through with her sacred sacraments including sadly, the untimely and unpredicted death of her father. So, it was totally out of her hands that when friends her age were searching for those ever so perfect white dresses with their moms, Keki had her hands full with other priorities such as making sure that her kids remembered and honored their father. Therefore, her religious commitment was put on hold until much later.

"She's finally going to do it!" My sister called me full of excitement.

"What are you talking about?"

"Mitzy, she's finally going to get to pick out her special dress, walk up to the altar, get anointed in Holy water, and receive her First Holy Communion. She's so excited; she's been waiting for this for so long."

Keki was so happy for her baby. The youngest of three, she was the only one who had never been baptized as a baby. Timing plays an important part, and in Keki's case it was everything. Too many obstacles had gotten in the way, but now the timing was perfect. This was Maritza's time. When her friends were getting ready to get confirmed during their sophomore year, our sweet little Mitzy was not only going to get confirmed, but she was going to receive her First Communion and get baptized all at the same time.

"Wow! For a minute there it sounded like a wedding! I've never heard of that."

Is that new or what? I wish the boys could have done something like that. Out of four, only one had completed his confirmation. The oldest was pretty much born a liberal so he always questioned everything including why he had to be confirmed when he was a sophomore in high school. Our second son, Joshua, thank God was confirmed on schedule when he was supposed to be, with a *padrino*, a celebration, a new suit, and a picture with the priest. Mark and Paul still have a chance to complete their confirmations before graduation.

"Are you sure she's going to do everything at the same time?" As I was talking to Keki, I was confused because all of this was something that we had never done before.

"She's doing the deluxe package! Some of the kids are doing one or two sacraments, and a few are doing all three at the same time, like Mitzy, so that's the deluxe package."

Well, whatever she called it, the super deluxe, number three, or trifecta, Maritza was excited to legally enter into the Catholic Church family. The celebration was afoot. All I know is that our First Holy Communion was very different when we were kids, but actually Mitzy got the royal treatment with her package deal.

While living in Weslaco, I had been preparing for the second sacrament that all Catholics look forward to—my First Holy Communion. Growing up in the Catholic Church receiving your First Holy Communion is a major accomplishment that is celebrated with much festivity especially in our family. With Mexican American families some girl's dresses are even as elaborate as miniature wedding dresses. Girls dress up entirely in white with fancy long tulle dresses, veils, and sparkly rhinestone crowns on their heads. Hair is of course made up and fixed at the hairdresser. They carry a white bible with a white rosary in their hands that are also adorned with long white gloves. Most little girls are so completely adorned that they can barely walk with their big puffy dresses. Part of the tradition is that *padrinos* are carefully selected by the parents, and they usually give the girl or boy gifts such as a necklace with a crucifix. They remain important members of the family throughout the child's life.

Everyone attends the mass of the celebration and afterward there is a big party with all of the family and friends. In addition to having a *comida*, there is usually a big cake with the religious symbols of communion on it and hot chocolate is also served with it. Of course at the celebration pictures are taken with family and the *padrinos* to mark the big event. It is a daylong event compared to a wedding and very special for everyone in the family.

I was preparing for this special event and every week Mommy made sure that I and the rest of my brothers and sisters attended CCD classes at our church. Usually we had to get a ride with someone because Mommy hardly ever had a car. I had to go on Wednesday, so I would often get a ride with my best friend Daniela because she was preparing to make her communion as well. If I couldn't go with her, I would walk all the way down 6th street, past the hospital, past the city pool, past the trailer park, past the VFW, past the high school, past the Baptist Church, past downtown, past the retirement home, until finally out of breath, thirsty, and tired I'd make it to the church. CCD classes would start and then it was usually walk back home again. It was during these classes that I was supposed to learn my prayers.

"The Church is making a change and instead of making your communion this year you will only do your first confession and then next year you will do your communion."

Mrs. Garcia announced to our second-grade class before we were about to go into the church to pray our prayers. She volunteered to be our teacher because two of her daughters were in our class, but we didn't mind because she was like a mom to all of us. Tall and pretty like a fashion model; Mrs. Garcia always dressed in fashionable styles and would tell me that I looked nice sometimes because I usually wore dresses.

"Why do you always wear dresses? You still wear shorts under them."

My friend Daniela asked me while looking at me like I was an object in a display case.

"I know, but I like wearing dresses, and I don't care if I have to wear shorts."

That was the rule. If we were to wear dresses, they had to be accompanied by shorts underneath. Girls couldn't leave the house without them or else they might have their dress pulled up by some mean boy. This rule applied everywhere, even at CCD.

"Daniela, do you know your prayers by memory?"

I was holding her hand as we were walking down the snakelike sidewalk that led into the side entrance of the church; I in my dress with shorts underneath and Daniela in her faithful stretchy striped pants with matching top. We were supposed to pray the Hail Mary and Our Father before our teacher to make sure we were ready to confess to Father Ian next week.

"I know them, you don't?"

"Well, I get nervous. I'm scared to talk to the priest. What if he gets mad at me? I'll forget my prayers and then he'll get real mad."

"Look, just pretend."

Daniela tried to make me feel better and told me just to make something up.

"What should I do?"

"Just say whatever, and if you forget your prayers act like you're saying them by mouthing them. No one will be able to tell."

Daniela was so smart; that's why she was my best friend. We practiced our prayers with our other friends. Since I didn't know mine very well, I watched Daniela. I figured no one could tell what I'm saying, so I'll mumble and pretend to be praying.

"Psst psssst pssst psssst," I continued to pretend to say my prayers while everyone else was praying. Daniela bent her head over next to mine and started to laugh.

"What are you doing?"

"I'm praying. Well pretending."

"You can't pretend to pray. You have to know the prayers."

"But I don't know them." She kept laughing at me. "You have to learn them by next week or you won't be able to do your confession."

Mrs. Garcia was walking by so we kept praying.

"Pssst pssst psst pssst pssst"

She couldn't tell that I didn't know them I told Daniela, so it doesn't matter.

"Okay kids, see you next week. Be ready for your confession."

We walked out of the church with Daniela still laughing at me and then her mom came to pick us up.

Wednesday came again and it was time for CCD. Daniela came for me again and this time was the day for our confession with the priest.

"Daniela, are you ready for confession?"

"I'm ready." She was very confident.

"What are you going to say?"

"Hmmm I can't tell you, but I do know."

"Remember what I told you; if you don't know what to say just make something up."

Before we knew it, we were in front of our church. We slid out of the small blue car and ran into our CCD class. Excited to see what our teacher would tell us we sat in our desks with our friends.

"Quickly class, Mrs. Garcia clapped her hands together. We don't have much time today because Father Ian has to listen to all of your confessions. Let's not keep him waiting. I hope you are all ready and you better remember your prayers." Before we received our First Communion, we had to confess and receive penance. She lined us all up as straight as an arrow and marched all down the sidewalk like soldiers to the side entrance of the church and sat us down in the first two pews of the church. One by one Mrs. Garcia took my friends to the dreaded confession booth. She had previously shown us the booth where the priest sat behind a black curtain like the Wizard of Oz, and we had to sit on the other side not being able to see him. I definitely felt like Dorothy.

We were supposed to say, "Forgive me Father for I have sinned."

Then, we had to tell him what we did wrong like we were on trial or something. That was going to be the hard part because we were supposed to remember everything that we did that we shouldn't have done. I know I shouldn't have done some things, but Father Ian didn't have time to listen to every little thing that I had to say.

One by one my friends were going into the scary closet. It seemed like something evil to me. How could something evil be in such a beautiful spiritual church? My heart was beating faster and faster as if I was about to be judged, and my future was on the line. What would my verdict be? How bad was I? Seven years old, could I be that bad? Daniela went next, and she didn't seem nervous. She was in the closet for less than a minute and went up to the front of the church to kneel down and pray.

Mrs. Garcia came right up to me, taking my hand saying "Okay *m'ijita*, your next."

Slowly I stood up shaking all over and wondering if I was the only one feeling this way. I clasped my sweaty hands, bent my head forward *persignando me*, took a deep breath, wanting to run and jump out the window like the lion but instead went forward into the closet.

Opening the door, I knelt down on the kneeler and said to the black curtain in front of me "Forgive me Father for I have sinned."

"So my little one, what is it that you have done?" The curtain replied in a nice voice sounding like Father Ian and trying to calm me down. He could tell I was nervous.

"¡Welllll!" I began, not knowing what to say and almost in tears. Then I remembered what Daniela told me.

"Make something up, just make something up!"

"I've been bad." I started.

"What did you do?" The voice asked.

"I hurt my friend, and I hurt my family, and I lied to my teacher." I quickly responded trying to get it over with.

"Is that all?" I knew Father Ian knew my parents, but I kept going hoping he couldn't recognize who I was. Then all of a sudden, I felt terrible.

"No, I'm lying to you because I don't know what to say."

Calmly he answered me. "Listen sweetheart, you shouldn't be scared, and you shouldn't lie about your sins. Just talk to me. It's your first time, and it will get easier with time."

I felt a little bit better, but not much better. I still felt like crying, but I asked the almighty OZ, "So can I go now?"

"Not quite yet." Then the voice told me to go to the altar and pray two Hail Mary's and two Our Fathers, and my sins would be forgiven just like that. I got up, opened the closet door, and Mrs. Garcia was waiting for me on the other side with a smile. I felt like Dorothy must have felt with a huge load lifted off of me and I wasn't shaking as much anymore. I walked to the front altar and knelt next to Daniela where she was praying. Looking at her, I bowed my head and formed the sign of the cross with my right hand, touching my forehead, my chest, my left shoulder, my right shoulder, then kissing my hand while at the same time saying, in the name of the Father, and the Son, and the Holy Spirit, Amen. This had become a natural habit now.

"Well?"

"I did it. I made up my confession because you told me to."

"You liar! I never told you to make anything up." I motioned to her with my finger to be quiet so that I could pray.

"Shhh," I said. Keeping my head bowed down.

"You see what you made me do; now I have to start over."

With my head down and Daniela giving me a mean glare, I began forming the sign of the cross with my right hand again starting over a bit slower this time. Finally I began with the Hail Mary.

"Hail Mary full of grace…"

Now with my confession behind me I was ready for my First Holy Communion. It was just my luck that we had moved from my hometown Weslaco, my Valley, my neighborhood, my church, to Houston. Everything was different and new including our church.

Mommy told me, "This church is very modern; they do things very differently than in the Valley. For your communion we'll be doing things the Houston way."

What did she mean? I was expecting the big celebration with the big white dress and cake, and *padrinos*. When I started going to CCD classes, the teacher confirmed my fears. Mrs.

Fort told the class that our First Holy Communion would be a simple sacrament.

"There is no need to make a big deal about this. Father does not want to distract from the regular mass, children. He wants for you to wear regular dresses, and you will take your communion along with the rest of the parish."

What a disappointment! I was so looking forward to this day and now it was just going to be a regular day. To top it off, we were away from all of our family.

"Mommy, I want to wear a white dress the way I'm supposed to wear!"

"The priest made it clear that you were not supposed to wear big white dresses. It has to be a simple dress and not white."

Mommy took me shopping and bought me a light blue dress with light pink flowers on it for my First Holy Communion. I did talk her into letting me wear Diana's old veil, but I hated my dress. Usually the *padrinos* help to choose the veil or will buy a gift for their godchild, but we were also told that we were not supposed to have *padrinos* either. Therefore, I didn't have *padrinos* for my First Holy Communion like my siblings did. After mass, Mommy took one picture of me in my blue dress in front of the church and, then we went home without a celebration, a cake, and *padrinos*.

P*apa* Maximiliano Gets Sick

Mommy got that dreaded phone call. *Papa* Maximiliano was very sick, so sick that he was not going to get better.

My parents packed everything up and headed back to the Valley, back to the family. At that time our house was being rented to my cousins who had come back from up north. Apparently *Papi* had made a deal with his sister while we were in Houston; they would stay in our house and take care of it while we were gone. Now we didn't have a place to stay, so we had to rent a house in Weslaco.

This house was right next to a *tiendita*, and we called it the rented house. I hated this house. It was a sad house because Mommy was hardly ever there; she was always at the hospital with *Papa* Maximiliano. Even though it was much newer than our house, and it had a carport, I still hated it. It felt weird to live there. Usually, it was only the five of us kids that were there. *Papi* was working and Mommy was with *Papa* Maximiliano at the hospital. She would come home and cry and go back to the hospital again.

Meanwhile, we had joined the church choir again with my *Tío* Betos' girlfriend Elena. She was the director of the choir and had recruited all of us to sing. Before we went to Houston we were in the choir, but now that we were back, Elena had asked us to go back and be part of the children's church choir. Being part of the choir was fun because Elena would take us and bring us back home. She would usually take us to get ice cream or *raspas* after practice also. Elena was extra nice to us not only because she was our uncle's girlfriend, but also, she was just nice to everyone. I loved going places with her. Whenever we were with her we would get extra attention because she was so pretty with long reddish hair and green eyes. What really made her beautiful was her personality and how she treated everyone so kindly.

In the choir we only sang Spanish songs. We got to wear beautiful white robes that flowed all the way down to the floor at mass and made us feel like angels. Only Keki, Eli, and I ended up going back. Johnny and Diana thought they were too old to join. Elena would pick us up and bring us back home from practice. After practice, we would walk to the *tiendita* and buy an ice cream and walk back home through the trail that was easily visible in the tall grass. This went on for a few months until one day Mommy came home with a blank look on her face and told us—*Papa* Maximiliano had died.

My grandfather, "*El Músico*," so light skinned with eyes as blue as the summer sky had died. Whenever we would go to see him, and we'd all walk into his tiny frame house he'd always sing, "*Ay viene, La América del Norte La América del Sur.*"

My little sister would run up to him, and he'd mess up her little golden curls. I was always so jealous, what about me? My hair was as straight as a board, and I hated it. *Papa* Maximiliano would sing this to Keki because her hair was blonde and in curls and she was so light-skinned. My hair and skin was also light, but not blonde like hers. None of that mattered though because my grandfather, *Papa* Maximiliano, had given me the best gift of all, my Lobo. Now he was gone. His blue eyes were no more. We could not look into his eyes when he'd play his violin to us anymore. Would the music at my grandparents' house stop, no more *músicos*? This was the first time someone in my family had ever died. It was the first time that I had seen Mommy so upset and cry so much that it scared me.

I watched her as she went into her closet and one by one gathered all of her dresses. She took them off of the hangers and put them into the bathroom sink. Pulling the sink stopper she plugged it to make sure that water could not escape and then turned the water on. Then she opened a box of Rit black dye and poured it into the sink. Getting all of her clothes, she put them in the bathroom sink and dyed them with Rit black dye. She repeated this with all of her clothing. Everything she wore after that was black—everything!

"Mommy, why are you doing that? You're scaring me." As I watched her dye her clothes black while she pushed back her tears, she tried to talk to me.

"When someone you love dies you do what you think you need to do to honor that person and to mourn him. This is what I need to do."

We were not allowed to watch TV or listen to the radio. Mommy was in mourning. We were all in mourning. This was a terrifying time for me especially when we all went to see my grandfather at the funeral home. I did not know what to expect. I had never been to a funeral home before. My parents told us that we were going to see him in his coffin and say goodbye to him, and we had to pray for him. We had to dress entirely in black. Why? Why did we have to do all of this?

As we arrived at the funeral home, many people were standing outside talking because there was no room inside. Some men were huddled in small groups smoking, and they approached *Papi* to say hello to him as we entered. We saw all of my cousins, my *tías*, *tíos*, and everyone that we knew,

120

crowded into the small chapel-like building as if they were filling an auditorium to watch a performance. The church-like pews lined up in rows with everyone sitting shoulder to shoulder, as the smell of incense mixed with coffee and *pan dulce* permeated the halls. My stomach ached with knots, and I felt like throwing up. How could anyone want *pan dulce*?

I saw my cousin Jimmy storming out of the chapel crying and upset about *Papa* Maximiliano, and I got even more nervous about going up to the front to see him in his coffin. All of the *tías* and *tíos* and Mommy and *Mama* Jesusa were sitting in the very front, right in front of the big ugly coffin, surrounded by all types of beautiful, colorful flowers. Usually flowers look and smell so pretty, but these made me feel sick. I had a glimpse of everything from the back of the chapel. Cries could be heard echoing and bouncing off the walls of the funeral home as some awful organ music played in the background. *Papi* said he would take all of us to the front to "*Dar* our *pesar*" to all of them, but I didn't want to go.

"You have to go see *Mama* Jesusa."

"No, I don't want to get close to him like that, I can't." He took the others to the front, and I waited in the back.

Later, Mommy came to the back to get me and told me that it was all right; I didn't have to see him if I didn't want to.

"I don't want to see him like that Mommy." I remember when he gave me Lobo and named him for me. He had so many grandchildren, but he gave me Lobo. I felt so special. That night I knew that I hated funeral homes. Many of my cousins went to the back where I was, and it was better with them around me. We sat in the back while we all prayed the *Rosario* that seemed to take forever. First, we would pray the Our Father, then ten Hail Mary's, then someone would sing and say some prayer, and then we'd repeat. It was all done in Spanish of course. "Why do we have to do this?" I'd ask my cousin.

"We always do this at funerals; it's a tradition." After what seemed like hours of "*Santa María*," the *tías* and *tíos* finally started to say their goodnights to my *Papa* Maximiliano and again the yells and cries could be heard coming out of the funeral home. When everyone left, we went back home, changed from our black clothes, and I cried myself to sleep.

The Present

I hated going back to our house on Mesquite Drive after we came back from Houston because we weren't the ones living there my cousins were. We were living in the rented house, the one with the *tiendita* next to it. It was a nice house, but it wasn't our house.

Papi said, "We need to give your *primos* time to move out. Your *tía* and *tío* are looking for a place to move to."

It was hard to imagine my *Tía* Lala and *Tía* Chencho and my cousins, Fela, Alda, Julian, Lolly, and Avelina all living in my house. How could they be in my bedroom? It wasn't fair. "I want my room back *Papi*!"

"*M'ijita*, you have to understand these things. We never planned on coming back. We planned to stay in Houston. We have to be patient." *Papi* was always so calm and patient.

Mommy told us that my *Tía* Lala had called for us to go over because she was having a party for Alda's birthday. She was a year older than me. Saturday came, and all of us got dressed up to go over to our house for my cousins' party. It was so weird to go to our own house and see other people there in our living room, in our kitchen, in our backyard. There were so many people there because our cousins from *Papi*'s side of the family were there, but also all of Alda's cousins from her family were there. We didn't know most of those kids. Her cousins were smart alecks and looked at us funny like we were from another planet or something. They didn't want to play with us or even try to make friends with us.

"Sometimes kids think that they're better than you for some reason,"*Papi* said.

All of the kids ran outside to gather around the pink princess *piñata* that my *Tío* Chencho had hung from one of the tall branches of our China Berry trees. He was holding the rope and pulling it so that the pink papier-mache doll would sway in the wind back and forth, back and forth teasing us. *Tía* Lala lined all of the kids up with the smallest to the tallest and made us back up so that we'd give enough room for the *piñata* to be hit. Alda would get to hit it first since it was her birthday. My *tía* blindfolded her with a pink bandana and spun her around three times, then placed the big decorated broomstick in her hands for her to swing with. She walked her over to the *piñata,* and with her hands holding Alda's hands she placed them on the *piñata* and tapped it three times.

"Do you feel that?"

"Yes, I feel it."

"Okay, then, go!"

"SWING!" She would start, as my *tío* would pull the rope and the *piñata* would fly up into the sky barely missing being hit.

"ONE," everyone would yell, "TWO," again my *tío* would keep pulling on the rope loving how the princess would jump back and forth, but escape its inevitable destiny..."THREE!"

"*Ya, m'ijita* let someone else go."

"I hardly got to hit it."

"After everyone hits it, then you can hit it again."

"But I want to break it; it's my *piñata!*"

Now the little kids would get to hit the princess, and they wouldn't even get blindfolded because they could hardly even hit. The babies went by fast and then the smaller kids, and the princess barely got a dent in her, but then the bigger boys at the end of the line came up to bat, and my *tío* started sweating bullets.

"*Haber*, Toni, (that's who the family called *Papi*) come help!"

One of Alda's cousins that we didn't know was going up to hit the princess, and he started to hit the ground with the broomstick saying, "Okay missy—watch out!"

My *tía* blindfolded and spun him around six times. Then my *tío* pulled the rope all the way up and dropped it all the way down to trick him, but it didn't work. As soon as he pulled it back up, this cousin got so fuming mad at the princess that he smacked her in her belly so hard that her legs went flying across the yard one way, and her head went and landed clear in the other direction.

"¡¡¡¡YAAAAAY!!!!" Everyone started screaming and running and all you could see was a mob under where the princess used to be.

"Those are mine."

"I got those." Everyone was grabbing as much candy as they could fit into their pockets and small bags. This was the absolute best part of the *piñata* even if it meant getting elbowed or trampled for some bubble gums; it was worth it.

"Now let's go sing Happy Birthday to Alda."

Running, all the kids raced inside. The kitchen table was the finish line, and they became the track stars where they had seen the decorated birthday cake with all of the presents surrounding it. We all gathered around and sang to my cousin, and then my *tía* cut the cake so that we could all eat some. Then the part that Alda had been dying for finally came. The presents! It was time to open the presents. All the cousins that we knew and the stuck-up ones that we didn't know gathered around her as we all watched eagerly wishing we could have all of those presents. One by one, Alda started to open each of her gifts. First present was a Barbie, and she liked it. Second gift was a doll, and she liked it too. Third gift was a board game, and she liked that one as well. Her next gift was cash, and of course she liked that. The gifts continued for a while, and I was wondering when our gift would come because I wasn't sure what we had gotten her. It had to be a good one because Mommy had gone downtown to look for a gift for her, and *Papi* said that she had gone to Wells of Weslaco to buy it. Wells was the best and most exclusive store in Weslaco and the Valley. That store was only for extremely special occasions because it was very expensive.

"Wow!" I thought. I couldn't believe that Mommy actually went to buy Alda a birthday gift at Wells of Weslaco. She doesn't even buy us anything there, but *Papi* said that she had to, so I'm sure that it will make Alda feel very special.

Finally, after opening many gifts Alda got to our present. She said, "This one is from *Tío* Toni & *Tía* Eliza". You could see the fancy wrapping and Wells of Weslaco label on the present, and I was so proud because we were giving her a present from that store. Alda quickly tore it open, and in the box was more fancy tissue papers which she threw out, and inside the tissue paper she found the most beautiful girl's panties in all different colors with exquisite lace.

"PANTIES!!!!" She yelled. "YOU GOT ME PANTIES!!!! I HATE THEM!!!! HOW COULD ANYONE GET ME PANTIES!!? I WANTED TOYS!!!" She grabbed the panties and threw them across the room and ran out crying.

Mommy started to cry as well. *Papi* followed Alda and

in front of everyone told her, "Apologize to your *tía*; when you receive a gift you say thank you. It doesn't matter if you don't like it. It doesn't matter if the gift is panties. You always say thank you."

Alda went up to Mommy with her head down and tears still in her eyes. "*Tía*, thank you for the panties."

Just Dance

Besides my grandfather and my teacher, another person that I knew who died was the boy who I almost danced with at my first dance. It was the summer after junior high school and I had always had the biggest crush on him. I know that he had one on me too because he told me so, and he would call me on the phone every day. At my house it was a battle to talk on the phone because I had to fight my sister for it every day, and it would usually get ugly between us. One-time *Papi* had to come in and rip the phone right out of the wall.

"Now no one gets to talk," he said. It took a while to fix that phone.

It was a quarter till eight and Bert and I were waiting in the junior high parking lot for our youngest of our four sons to come out of the gym. He had his first real dance, and my husband and I were both excited for him, hoping that it had gone well for him. Kids were starting to pour out of the building like it was the last day of school with a dazed look on them as they waited for their rides. We didn't want to be too obvious, having had experience with our other three boys we waited for him to come to us.

I had learned the hard way with my oldest that standing up on the step of my SUV and waving my arms in the air as I shouted, "Over here Sweetie, I'm over here," was not the best way to win over my thirteen-year-old son.

"Mom! Don't ever do that again! You just embarrassed me in front of the entire school!"

Well, how is a mom supposed to know that her son doesn't want everyone in the school to hear his mom calling him "Sweetie?" Now, by the fourth son we had it down. We were going to play it cool, park, and wait for our son Paul to find us in the parking lot. No big deal.

After a minute my cell phone buzzed, "Mom, where are you?" He does need me after all.

"We're in the parking lot—the first row." It was such a great feeling to know that he was calling right away.

"I'll be right there." In a minute our baby jumps into the back seat as sweaty as can be.

"Hey, baby did you have fun?" Out of breath he begins to tell us his adventures of his first dance.

"Mom, you know how you always tell us that if we're going to go to a dance you don't want us just holding up a wall, that you want for us to dance?" I just looked at him and both my husband and I smiled. "Well, I danced the entire dance!"

Mommy had five sisters, the *tías*, and they were all extremely close that not a day went by that they didn't talk on the phone or see each other in person. All but one, *Tía* Lena lived in Weslaco, but that didn't matter because they all stayed in touch daily. From all of those *tías*, two of them had daughters exactly my age. I mean exactly to the same month. Our moms were pregnant together! Throughout our school years my cousins weaved in and out of elementary, junior high, and high school in the same class. We had several other cousins older and younger in school with us, but none of them were the exact age as these two *primas*.

Having Bibi and Lali in the same grade as I was both good and bad like a bittersweet candy. Everything that went on at school that we wanted our moms to know or not to know they knew automatically because one of us would tell them. Sometimes we would promise to not say anything to our moms and pinky swear to make sure that they wouldn't find out. Pinky swear was the ultimate of swears. If you did that then you were as good as gold. It wasn't that I was keeping anything from my mom, but her and her sisters seemed to overreact and create much more drama out of every little situation even when there was no reason. At times it was just best. One of the times was our very first dance.

Everyone knows that one of the most exciting parts of being in junior high school is going to your first dance.

"No. You can't go and that's that!" My dad said.

My mom went along with him. "Do you know what goes on at those dances? There's no way that you're going. You are way too young to dance anyway." Mommy was in the kitchen making dinner for all seven of us and hurriedly started tossing spices around as if she was a chef in a famous restaurant. I could tell that the subject bothered her. She'd pound the spices down in the *molcajete* with all of her might.

"But Mommy! I love dancing; you know I love dancing! Please let me go! I'm in student council, and we're sponsoring the dance. I have to go. It's my responsibility; I'm supposed to work at the concession stand."

My mommy had become a Charismatic Catholic and expected for all of us to follow what she believed as well. I too was a Christian, but that didn't keep me from loving to move when my favorite song came on the radio. I still loved to dance, and I also loved music.

"PLEASE, let me go to the dance! This is so important to me!"

By now the pots and pans were banging and Mommy was not even talking anymore, at least not to me. She was now rolling out the *tortillas*, tossing them on the *comal*, flipping them over with her bare hands then placing them on the table all in synchronized motion. I turned to *Papi* who was reading the newspaper. He usually read it in the morning, but sometimes he didn't have enough time because he had to take all of us to school, then get to work, and then he had classes at night. He put the newspaper down on the linoleum table and looked me right in my eyes.

"Look *m'ijita*. We're doing it for your own good. You'll understand later."

I burst into tears and ran into our room, not my room because I didn't have my own room. My sisters and I shared a room and a bed, so I ran into our room and jumped onto our bed and cried. Yes, I was only twelve years old, but it was a junior high dance, and I was in junior high. The student council was sponsoring the dance, and I was the seventh-grade vice president. Didn't any of that matter? I guess to my parents it didn't.

I buried my face into my pillow and cried thinking that I was so unlucky because I couldn't go to the dance. Everyone was going to go and have so much fun, but not me. I had to stay home, be bored, cry, and imagine everyone else dancing while I was at home sitting on the bed that I shared with my sisters. It just wasn't fair. Before I knew it, night had turned to morning and it was time to get up and get ready for school. Apparently, I had cried myself to sleep.

Mommy was driving us to school in the blue bat mobile this morning. "Please, Mommy drop me off here." I always made her drop me off before the entrance of the junior high so that no one could see our embarrassing old-fashioned car with points above each rear light. It was bad enough that my mom had to take my little sister and little brother along to drop me, but the car, please.

"*¡Ay qué niña!*" Mommy says, as I get off. While I approached the entrance, I spotted my *primas* in a group with other girls, so I went over to them.

"Well, what did she say about the dance?"

They both looked at me anxiously as if they were waiting to hear the winning number to the lottery.

"I can't go." I said with my head down and trying not to cry.

"Are you serious? What do you mean you can't go? We can only go if you go, and we told our moms that you were going so you have to go."

"They said I couldn't." I answered them back sternly because they didn't seem to understand what I was saying.

"No, listen to us. You have to go because we are not going to miss this dance. Do you know who is going to be there?"

Bibi looked at me and grabbed my arm.

"Elias is going to be there, and there is no way that I am going to miss this opportunity because of you."

Then Lali grabbed my other arm and started in on me. "Everyone is going to be there, and they expect me to be there too. I've told them that I will go, and I'm not going to let them down. You better come up with a plan."

The dance was in a few days, and I had to do something because I couldn't have my favorite cousins mad at me forever.

"Fine, I'll ask them again. I'll tell them I need it for a grade."

They seemed happy now.

"What difference does it make? None of us are allowed to dance anyway."

They both looked at me like I was from another planet.

"Are you crazy?"

All three of our moms believed the same way. It was plain evil and sinful. We were like the kids from *Footloose*, except it was for real.

"Que lo mande Dios, vale más que no sepamos que ustedes están bailando porque les va ir muy mal."

Mommy and my *tías* would always tell us. If we were to dance and they'd find out we'd get in deep trouble. I know I didn't want to find out what would happen.

Now I had to approach my parents again and let them know that I had to go to this dance, and I had to sort of lie to them to make sure that they'd let me go. While I was helping Mommy with dinner and *Papi* was sitting at the kitchen table reading the daily newspaper, I decided to go for it.

"Mommy, *Papi*, I know we already talked about the dance, but our student council sponsor was telling us at our meeting that if we don't go to work the concession stand then we will not be able to go on the end of the year field trip to the Grapefruit Bowl in Mission. I've been working really hard for that trip, and I want to go. It won't be fair if I don't get to go just because I don't go to this dance. I'm not going to dance, I promise—just work. Bibi and Lali are going to go. We'll be fine Mommy. Nothing will happen. Please! Please let me go!"

Mommy put her spatula down next to the stove and turned to *Papi*, his head buried in the newspaper.

"*Papi*, didn't you hear what I said?"

He put the newspaper slowly down and looked at Mommy.

"You know how I feel about these dances." She told him. He looked at me.

"Please *Papi*, I promise I won't dance!" He looked at Mommy as if to want to give in, but held back a bit.

"Let us think about it; we'll let you know later."

Let me know later. Well, at least it wasn't a straight-out no. I still had a chance. After that I tried my best to do everything perfect so that they would notice how good I was being. Maybe they would give me an answer but nothing. It was like waiting for the nurse to give you an injection, but it never happens. You know it's coming, just not sure when. Finally, it was time to go to bed. All of us were taking showers and getting ready when *Papi* called me into the sacred room—my parents' bedroom.

"You can go, but absolutely no dancing. The condition that we are letting you go is because you have to work for student council; otherwise, we wouldn't allow it. You will have to go with your cousins because they are not allowed to dance either. Do you understand?" *Papi* had a stern but quiet way of talking to us. He didn't raise his voice, but was always heard loud and clear.

"Perfectly!" I said as I jumped up and gave him a big hug and Mommy too for permitting me. "Thank you! Thank you! I won't let you down."

The next morning at school, I begged Mommy to drop me off a block away so that no one would see me; they were waiting for me in the front.

"Well?"

I pretended that I didn't know what they were talking about just to make them mad.

134

"Well, what?"

They were both fuming because the dance was already that night, and I knew that they had their dresses ready.

"Elias's friend just told me that he asked if I was going, and I said I was. So, you are going aren't you?"

Both of them stood with their hands on their hips and a look like I was the witness and they were the prosecutors.

"Hey, wait a minute. Y'all need me remember? You should be nice to me instead of eating me up like some shark. Why don't you try being nice to me instead of attacking me?"

"Fine, we'll be nice!" As they start tickling me, "Here's your nice!"

Giggling uncontrollably I say, "Stop! Stop! I'll tell you—they said I could go!"

Simultaneously they drop me. All of a sudden, they forget that I'm even there and get so excited talking about the dance.

"Wait a minute; we can't dance! Did y'all hear me! We can't dance!"

They didn't listen to me, or they didn't want to hear me because they kept talking about what they were going to wear, and who was going to be there, and the different songs they were going to dance to, etc…

"STOP! WE CAN'T DANCE!"

Finally they heard me and looked over at me with a—are you out of your mind look.

Lali comes right up to me looking me straight in my eyes that our wireframe glasses almost got tangled up.

"Do you think that we are actually going to go to a dance and not dance?"

They know that our moms do not want for us to dance and that those are the conditions, so why are they asking me that.

"We can't go unless we agree not to dance. I promised my parents." Lali and Bibi look at each other and burst out laughing.

"Fine, then we won't dance either."

As they walk away together laughing uncontrollably, I stay there thinking that they couldn't possibly mean that they would disobey their moms, our moms. I knew that if one of us got in trouble, we would all get in trouble.

Finally, the night of the big dance was upon us. Of course, I was nervous knowing everyone would be there, but I didn't have anything new to wear so I'd just have to wear my usual church dress. I would dress it up with my knee-high socks, and wear my long hair pulled back with a fancy barrette, and add ribbons. It was a fashionable mini dress after all, and fixing my hair was something that I liked doing, and I was pretty good at it too. Lali, Bibi, and I had agreed that we would all go together so they were going to come over early, and Mommy and *Papi* were going to take us and pick us up.

The doorbell rings. "They're here!"

I was so excited that I completely forgot that my dress wasn't zipped up in the back. They started laughing at me when I realized that my zipper was not up, and I got mad at them.

"Well don't just stand there, zip me!"

They were both dressed in cute mini dresses with of course the signature knee-highs.

"We better hurry; I want to get there early." Bibi quickly says.

"I'm the one who needs to be there early; remember I need to work there." I remind them why we are even going.

"We know, we know. Go call your parents so we can go, they order me." I run to my parents' bedroom to tell them that we're ready to go, and they start to follow me.

"We'll be right back!" They yell out to Johnny who is in the backyard with my other brother and sisters. With that we go out the front door and the three of us, Bibi, Lali, and I get into the Batmobile along with Mommy and *Papi*. We can hardly contain our excitement, when *Papi* bursts our bubble.

"You all realize that we are taking you to this dance, but you have to stay together, and we are not allowing Suzy to dance. She does not have our permission. The only reason she is going is to work. We understand that the two of you are not going to dance either because you don't have permission either. Is that right?"

I look at them, and they look at each other. Then they both say, "That's right."

As we approach the junior high, he parks right in front of the gym door as everyone is going inside.

"Alright then, we'll pick you all up here at 10 o'clock sharp."

We said our goodbyes and jumped out of the Batmobile. They waited until we went inside. It was so embarrassing. As we walked inside I felt so happy that I was allowed to be a part of this great dance. All of the popular music was playing loudly, and the gym had been decorated with streamers of bright colors and balloons. On one side of the gym were bleachers where a bunch of girls were sitting down just hoping that someone would come over and ask them to dance. Some people were standing at the edge of the dance floor. Then on one side were all of the guys that seemed to be holding up the wall, just standing there staring at everyone. At the far end were four tables set up with posters, which made up the concession stand. That was where I had to go.

"I'm going to have to go with the student council to work, so I guess I'll see y'all later unless you want to come over and help me."

"Are you kidding? We're going to go talk to our friends and see what's going on."

They started to walk over in the opposite direction where all of the crowds were near the bleachers.

"Remember, y'all can't dance." All I heard was laughing.

I walked over to the concession stand where all of my student council buddies were. It was pretty crowded in there that they made some of us leave. Apparently, everyone had shown up wanting to work. The sponsor said I'd have to come back in a while. Listening to the music was fine with me. I'll stand here and observe, listen to the music, and watch everyone else have a good time. As I stood there watching everyone dance on the dance floor, I could feel my feet move. I couldn't help it; they were dying to dance and join in. Why is this so hard for me? All I have to do is stand here. Don't move. But as much as I tried, my feet would move to the music. Then, I felt a tap on my shoulder.

"Dance with me." I turned around and saw him smiling at me.

"I can't." I smiled back at him.

"You know you want to. I saw your feet moving. Come on. Dance with me."

Again, I look at him smiling. "I can't."

He stands there next to me for a while. His eyes are the greenest eyes that you can look right through them like windows when you're gazing outside. He's the same boy who comes to mow the lawn next to our house sometimes, and I panic when I see him. Why can't I say—sure I'll dance with you? What could be the harm in that? Why do my parents have to be so darn strict? Do they even realize how important this is to me, and how they are ruining everything for me? I'm the only person in the entire junior high who is not allowed to dance, that is not going to dance that is. Even if I did dance with him, how would they know? My cousins—that's how. They would somehow tell my *tías* and my mom would surely find out. That would be the worst ever. He looks over at me again. Now they're playing another song. I love this song. Should I tell him the truth? Would he believe me?

"Please, let's dance."

He's taking my hand and pulling me onto the dance floor. What am I supposed to do? His brown hair is long and feathered just above his shoulders. He's wearing a striped terry cloth shirt with Levi blue jeans and brown desert boots.

"Look, I know you probably don't believe me, but I'm not allowed to dance."

"Is it against your religion? If it is, I understand."

"No, it's not that. I guess it would make more sense if it were my religion, but it's just that it's against my parents. They won't let me, and I promised them that I wouldn't disobey them."

He smiled at me again. "That's nice of you. I like that. Not too many kids would do that. I mean, they would say one thing, then do another."

He stayed there next to the concession stand and talked to me the entire night. While I worked, he stood next to the concession stand and didn't dance at all. He could have danced with any girl, but he didn't. The dance was fun even though I didn't dance.

Meanwhile my *primas* were sweating up a storm on the dance floor all night long. They would come over to the concession stand, give me an evil glare, quickly pick up their knee-highs', and dash right back onto the dance floor.

"They're picking us up in a few minutes!" I'd yell.

I had to remind them that we would be leaving soon because they were having way too much fun to remember. Finally, I had to go and practically drag them off of the dance floor so that we could get ready to leave.

"We have to go!"

As we started to walk out to the Batmobile, all I could hear them say was, "You better not say a word! Pinky Swear!"

Earrings

Being the mom of four boys has been a challenge. Two years apart they're best friends one minute, and the next I find them wrestling each other on the floor. Yes, they're a challenge. They're rough, tough, messy, and boy they love to eat all of the time. For being boys though, you would think that the tough *"Macho"* attitude that is usually seen in our Mexican American culture would have been passed down to them, but when it comes to needles, all of them run like tiny scared kittens being chased by a mean old pit bull. They hate shots, doctor's offices, can't stand the sight of even the tiniest bit of blood, etc…

"You guys would have never made it as a girl!" Driving home from the doctor's office all of them are complaining because they had to get immunizations for back to school.

"What's the matter with y'all?" I can't understand that my sons are already teenagers and still terrified of needles.

"Mom, the pain—it hurts so much, and it even bled. You heard the doctor, he said it would hurt." My drama queen Mark tries to explain his behavior to me as I turn the knob of the radio down to listen to his elaborate dramatization of what had transpired.

"Babe, you didn't have to run down the hall and make the nurse hunt you down like that. You're getting a little too old for that." As his brothers started laughing he turned to Joshua and smacked him on his shoulder then of course Joshua smacked him back.

"Hey, stop it guys! Y'all have no idea what girls have to go through or some guys for that matter just to look good. Did you know that if all of you were girls I would have probably had the doctor punch holes in your earlobes as soon as you were born?"

Suddenly, they stop hitting each other. Paul the youngest one seems the most concerned and asks me "Mommy, why would you do that?"

"Baby, don't worry about it because I didn't have to do it. All of you were boys, thank God."

"But Mom, that's plain wrong to do that to innocent babies when they don't even know whether they would want their ears pierced or not. You're deciding something for them that they should choose when they are old enough to make their own decision. Regardless of that, there are probably many health issues involved with piercing an infants' ears because the possibility of it getting infected are much higher at that age. How can people possibly do that?" Of course my oldest, our politician was always concerned for everyone's rights. He was born a liberal.

"Look Rigo that's our culture, you know that. I didn't create it; I was just born into it."

As we approach our house and I park in our garage the boys get out of the car complaining, Mark goes for one last stab at Joshua.

"Ouch! Don't punch me there—can't you see my Pokémon Band-Aid!" Yes, thank God I had boys. They would have never made it as girls—not in the world that we live in.

Most Mexican American baby girls are born into a beautiful and colorful culture that seems to dictate much of what one will be from the very start. Many of us come into

142

our world without choices in some areas. One of these choices would be whether to have your ears pierced or not. Usually shortly after a baby girl is born her ears are pierced with no questions asked. Parents do not wait until the child can make her own decision about wanting their ears pierced or not. Baby girl—boom, gold earrings, it's that simple. Yet, as soon as we were old enough, my sisters and I began questioning Mommy and *Papi* why they hadn't pierced our ears.

"How come I don't have pretty gold earrings?"

Looking at Mommy, I'd give her a sad face so that she'd know that I really wanted them.

"We just didn't think it was right for us to do that."

Didn't they know that having our ears pierced was one thing that we did want for them to do for us.

"Why wouldn't you do that for us, all of our *primas* have earrings and they all look so pretty!"

Having a large family was a great advantage because Mommy was one of ten siblings and *Papi* was one of eight. On Mommy's side alone we had over fifty first cousins.

"Every time we get together our *primas* always ask us why we're the only ones without pierced ears. We always have to be the different ones. Why couldn't you have just taken some earrings with you to the hospital when we were born and get it over with like everyone else did? It's just not fair!"

Crying and stomping I would protest to Mommy day after day until something major happened that changed everything. My sister Diana got her driving permit. Suddenly it was as if I had been given a key to the jewelry store.

"You have to do this for me. It's what I've wanted all of my life more than anything, and they don't understand. Please, I'll do anything for you…"

My sister was willing to be the accomplice in my little scheme, since she felt sorry for me. She wasn't the easiest to convince either because Diana was always getting after me for little things, since she was my big sister. Sometimes though, she'd just get tired of me bugging her and have to give in.

"Fine! I'll do it!"

I knew I was going to owe her big time, but I didn't care, it would be worth it if my ears had shiny gold earrings.

"Let's go ask *Tía* Chema."

Our *tía* lived across the street from us and happened to be extremely popular in our town. She knew everyone. *Papi* was her cousin, but we called her our *tía*. We knew that we could trust anything that she would tell us because she grew up with our dad and always said that she was just like his sister.

We knocked on her door, "*Pasen m'ijitas.*"

We walked inside where she was busy working in the kitchen. She was a great cook and a great baker.

"*Tía*, we know that you know everyone in town."

Smiling with approval we knew that we were on the right track.

"We came to ask you for an important favor. I need to get my ears pierced, but I don't want Mommy to know." She looked at me carefully and then looked at Diana.

"*Ay m'ijitas*, you don't have your ears pierced? ¿Por qué? ¡*No, No es justo!*"

Looking at us, she studied our bare faces as if we were specimens in a science laboratory. She seemed to wonder how it could be possible that Mexican American girls related to her had not only gotten away with but also escaped the traditional ritual. Why had our parents not allowed our ears lobes to be poked by a needle when we were babies—like normal parents?

"That's what we want to know, but we don't. Mommy and *Papi* don't want us to pierce them, but I'm going to do it anyway. Will you help me find someone to do it for me? Please!"

I gave her a sad face and looked at her as I pulled back my long hair and held my ear right up to her showing her how naked it seemed.

"*¡M'ijita, Ay Chihuahuas*! I can't go against your parents. ¡Your *Papi es como hermano*! But then again, all girls should have their ears pierced. You should have had them done a long time ago, and you wouldn't have felt a thing. Newborn babies can't even use their tiny hands to pull on their ears yet. It's easy, so easy. Now, well I don't know. I've heard it's harder the older you get. *Pero mira*, I know a lady… I'll tell you where you can go and then you decide if you want to do it or not."

She quickly turned and walked away, and I started to jump up and down not able to hold my screams that were about to come out of my mouth as Diana pulled me down to reality. Out of nowhere she returned with a paper as she started to jot a name and address down. Handing it to Diana, she started giving us directions.

"Her name is Toña, *Doña* Toña. Just tell her I sent you. Oh, and here—she's going to need these."

Tía Chema handed me a pair of gold stud earrings still in their original box that must have belonged to my cousin Elma.

"After she pierces your ears, she'll need earrings to place on your ears."

I was so happy that I just hugged her and said,

"Thank you! Thank you so much!"

Diana looked at me from the corner of her eyes as if I was some weirdo, not really wanting to look. Maybe I was overreacting a bit. How could I be overreacting? I was going to get what I wanted—holes punched in my ears.

She pulled me by my arm and said, "Let's go now." We said our goodbyes running out the front door.

"What's the matter with you? Do you have to act like a helpless puppy all of the time?"

She was always the general having to be in control. But what could I do; I needed her to drive me. So we were off to find Toña's house on the other side of town with my borrowed gold earrings in hand.

"Where is this house anyway?"

My sister knew more or less from the address that it was on the other side of town, but it would take us a while to find exactly where this *Doña* Tonya lived.

"It's got to be in this neighborhood."

Pointing towards the next street, I looked ahead at what was to come. Lining the street were rows of homes decorated with potted plants, statues of *La Virgen de Guadalupe*, and the occasional car parked on the front yard. In the distance we could hear someone's radio blaring some Tex-Mex *conjuntos* harmonizing with the barks of the dogs roaming the neighborhood. I looked down at the tiny box and opened it smiling at myself.

"Thanks for doing this for me. You know it means everything to me."

Yes, she was bossy, but she was my big sister and did everything for me.

"It doesn't mean everything to you. You don't even know what that means. How could having your ears pierced

146

possibly mean everything to you? You are so materialistic."
Yes, that's my sister.

"Still, you're helping me do it."

She kept looking at the small frame houses. We passed a pink, then a blue, then a white and yellow, then a green one, and then finally we spotted it.

"That's it!" Diana looked down at the paper that our *tía* had given us with the address.

"Yes, it's that one. The hot pink one with the big statue of The Virgin in front."

She pulled the car over to the curb as the dogs barked louder and started to circulate closer to us as if it was dinnertime, and we had their Alpo.

"Are you ready? You don't have to do this. We can go home. I don't know about this place." I opened the box again and showed it to her.

"I'm ready. I was ready when I was born."

We got out of the car ignoring the barking dogs. We were used to that kind of thing. The front door of the hot pink house was blocked off with plants, so we had to go around to the side door. We passed The Virgin that was surrounded by some altar and beautiful red roses all around her.

"Wow! That's beautiful." Diana was mesmerized by the serenity of the statue.

Living in the Valley, we were used to seeing statues like this one as well as those of Jesus and saints in people's yards.

"Maybe that's a good sign."

We walked up to the side door as the scent of freshly made flour *tortillas* mixed with freshly brewed coffee caught our noses. Knock-knock-knock…

"*¿Quién es?*" A voice from the other side of the door asked us who we were.

"Our *Tía* Chema sent us to get our ears pierced." I yelled at her through the screen door.

Bang, bang, clank, clank. She put some pots or pans away and came up to the screen door.

"Chema *la de* Tiko?"

Tiko was my *Papi's* uncle who was even more well-known than our *tía*.

"Yes, she said that you could help us."

She lifted up the rusty hook that kept the screen door closed and slowly opened the squeaky door.

"*Pasen.*" Looking at each other Diana gives me the eyes as if to say you first.

"*Gracias.*"

We both walk into the tiny kitchen where a small Formica table and three mismatched chairs hug the wall.

Doña Toña pulls out a chair and says "*Siéntense niñas.*"

Diana and I sit down as she leaves the kitchen and quickly returns.

"*¿Quién quiere aretes?*"

I waste no time and tell her "*Yo, quiero aretes.*"

There was no reason to spend time on chit-chat; I was there for one purpose, and I wanted to get it over with.

She then looked over at Diana and asked her "*Y tú?*"

Diana shook her head to signal that she did not want anything done to her. "No thank you."

Doña Toña looked at me and asked "*¿Trajistes aretes?*"

Thank goodness *Tía* Chema had given me the box of earrings to bring because I had never owned a pair before.

"*Tienen que ser de oro.*"

On top of that now Ms. Toña is telling me that the earrings have to be pure gold. *Tía* Chema said that they were gold. I hope she meant that they were pure gold. I handed her the box, and she opened it and looked at Elma's earrings.

"*Muy bien. Te va a costar dos* dollars."

Two dollars! I didn't have money. Diana got her purse and took out two dollars to give Toña.

"Here…" Toña took the money and laid it on the table.

She pulled the earrings from the box and separated the studs from the backs, laying them on the table. Then she went to the freezer and took out an ice cube. That's weird I thought. What does she need an ice cube for? Just as I was thinking that I felt the ice on my earlobe. As I looked over at Diana with a "What the…" expression, she had an alarmed and disgusted look of fear on her face like we better run for our lives now.

When suddenly, "Owww! What's that?"

Before anyone could even answer me, I saw *Doña* Toña pick up the gold stud and "OUCHHHHHHHHHHHH!!!!!!"

Just like that, she popped it through my earlobe. She didn't even use alcohol. Then she put the back on as the blood was squirting all over the place.

"*No se hace nada.*" It's no big deal she said, as she handed me a paper towel.

Then she went in for a second round. POP!—

"OUCHHHHHHHHHHHHHH!!!!!!!!"

The second was even worse than the first especially when the blood started to ooze out as she placed the back on and then handed me another paper towel as if she was casually handing me an invitation.

"OK…*Ya estás lista.*"

Diana quickly got up and opened the screen door, scared that she might grab her ear next.

"That's it? *Es todo?*" I looked at *Doña* Toña confused and obviously still in pain with tears rolling down my face.

"*Ya m'ijita—no llores, no seas soflamera. Querías aretes, verda? Que te vaya bien.*"

Grabbing my hand, Diana pulled me out of the house.

"What's wrong with you? How could you have done that? She didn't even use alcohol!"

Holding the bloody paper towels to my ears I pulled them off to show her the shiny gold on my ears. We ran passed The Virgin and the pack of howling dogs that were waiting outside our car.

"Hurry and get in before these guys smell the blood on you."

As we shut the car door we both burst out laughing not believing what we had just gone through.

"You know what? I think I got some blood on The Virgin as we ran by her. Maybe we should go back and clean it." Diana gives me the look.

"Are you crazy?"

I pull the passenger visor down and look into the mirror at my bloody, shiny, gold earrings as she starts the car and begins to pull away from *Doña* Toña's house. I look over at her a bit out of breath, but somewhat concerned.

"Tell me the truth." Leaning over close to her, I pull my hair back and push my head to the side so that she can see my new earrings.

"How do they look? Of course you have to imagine them without the blood and swelling and everything, but really, how do they look?"

My sister keeps driving past the colorful array of houses and says nothing. As she pulls up to a stop sign she looks over at me.

"Let me see." I quickly shove my ear towards her again trying to ignore the pain that is throbbing throughout both my ears and head.

"I guess without all of that yucky blood and swelling they're fine for someone that is as materialistic as you and goes through *Doña* Tonya's torture for the sake of so called beauty." She drives off, and I sit back looking out of the window...

"Thanks for taking me, Di."

Again, she looks at my ears and then at me, smiling.

"You know what, on second thought, they look pretty good. Maybe we can bring Keki to get her ears pierced with *Doña* Toña."

Then we both burst out laughing.

Bibliography

Baum, L. Frank. *(1939)*. *"The Wizard of Oz."*

Brown v. The Board of Education, (1959).

Frost, R. (1923). *Nothing Gold Can Stay.*

Hinton, S.E. (1967). *"The Outsiders."* Vikings Press.

Serling, Rod. (1959). *"The Twilight Zone."*